'What is it, Marc?'

'I was just wondering if it was a good idea, my bringing you here tonight.' He tapped the steering-wheel absently as he spoke.

Becky gasped with surprise. 'Why?'

'Well, now you've seen that everything is unchanged, if we buy the property and start altering it, I'm going to be the villain of the piece.'

'As long as the alterations are within reason, I won't object.' Her excitement was dampened by his brooding attitude.

'Won't you? I wonder.'

Although a Lancastrian by birth, **Sheila Danton** has now settled in the West Country with her husband. Her nursing career, which took her to many parts of England, left her with 'itchy feet' which she indulges by travelling both at home and abroad. She uses her trips to discover new settings for her books, and also to visit their three grown-up children, who have flown the nest in different directions.

Recent titles by the same author:

THE FAMILY TOUCH
A GROWING TRUST

GOOD HUSBAND MATERIAL

BY
SHEILA DANTON

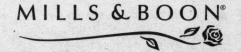

MILLS & BOON®

First published in Great Britain 1999
Harlequin Mills & Boon Limited,
Eton House, 18-24 Paradise Road, Richmond, Surrey TW9 1SR

© Sheila Danton 1999

ISBN 0 263 81943 4

Set in Times Roman 10½ on 12 pt.
03-0002-52597

Printed and bound in Spain
by Litografia Rosés S.A., Barcelona

CHAPTER ONE

SEATED on the low brick wall which flanked an incongruous pair of wrought iron gates, Rebecca Groom's blue eyes watched a black Labrador tug a tall man across the road. The dog was determined to reach the shade of the surgery building as soon as possible.

As she moved towards the safety of her baking hot, yellow Mini, allowing the heat of the sun to wash over her, she sympathised with the dog.

'Problem? Or are you just planning a break-in?' The man's craggy features filled her open window as she settled behind the wheel and she recognised the amused features of the practice senior partner. At the same moment, Marc Johnson gave a gasp of recognition.

'Well, if it isn't our new recruit. You weren't expecting to find the health centre open on a Sunday, were you?'

'No way,' she laughed. 'I've taken a flat at Begstone and am trying to work out how long I need to allow for the journey.'

'Begstone?' he raised his eyebrows in mock horror. 'It'll take you a lot longer than it took you today. That's just about the worst place you could live for rush-hour traffic!'

'Now you tell me,' she said with a laugh.

'It's not all doom and gloom, though.' He swept back a stray lock of straight, dark hair. 'There's a faint chance that the surgery may be moving a lot closer to Begstone.'

'There is? Where?'

'The idea's still very hush-hush, but if it'll prevent you

rushing back to tear up your tenancy agreement I suppose I can tell you. Especially as you don't know the area.'

'Well, I did—' Becky was about to confess she knew the area much better than he thought when he interrupted her.

'You're baking in there. Why don't we discuss this in a more civilised manner, over a cold drink?'

The invitation was tempting. Extremely so. The heat inside the Mini *was* unbearable. Sure she must look like a wilted flower, Becky swept a strand of damp auburn hair back with her fingers. If only she'd waited until later in the day to work out the best route to take the next morning. 'Sounds good.'

'I'll just return Sally to my mother at the end of the road. You can either leave the car here or park outside number twenty-three.'

'I think I'll try and find a shady parking spot over the road.'

He nodded approvingly. 'We walk very slowly. Sally is no longer in the first flush of youth.'

'How old is she?'

'Nearly twelve.'

'That's good for a Labrador.'

'She's not pure-bred, which probably accounts for it, but even Sally won't last much longer unless she gets more exercise than my mother gives her. When she comes out with me she has a shock. I'll see you at the end of the road.'

As she put the car in motion, she remembered how, at her interview, Marc's inscrutable expression had given little away, apart from a suggestion of near obsession about healthy eating and exercise. His own lean and muscular frame had not an ounce of spare flesh. Commendable really. but Becky had suspected he perhaps didn't take into account hereditary factors. However, despite the generous curves she had inherited from her mother, she had been offered the job, so perhaps she shouldn't worry.

Despite a certain tautness of his features, which excluded any hint of familiarity, he had certainly been courteous and friendly, both today and at the interview, making her feel he was someone she could work with harmoniously. *And* he cared about his mother. That merited definite bonus points!

She parked beneath the branches of a spreading chestnut tree and, having locked the car, waited for them to join her.

'I can't make Sally hurry in this heat.' The compassionate smile that accompanied his words softened his features, revealing a good-looking profile that hadn't been obvious to Becky before. Yet there was a reflective air about him that she couldn't quite put her finger on.

'It's too hot for any of us to be rushing about.'

When they reached his mother's house, he opened the gate and waited for her to precede him into the front garden. 'Mum will be in the back. We'll go round this way.' He freed Sally from her lead and indicated the leafy path at the side of the large stone-built house.

Mrs Johnson lifted her head to greet her son and when she saw Becky she leapt up in surprise. 'Hello…er…'

'Mum, this is Rebecca Groom—our new treatment room nurse. She starts tomorrow.'

'Hello. Pleased to meet you, Rebecca.'

'Good afternoon, Mrs Johnson. What a beautiful garden.' Becky surveyed the large acreage with admiration.

'Kind of you to say so, but these days I have to have help to keep it this way.'

It sounded as if she lived there alone and, judging by the faint sadness in her eyes as she spoke, Becky guessed she was probably a widow. As Marc's help wasn't mentioned, she presumed he had his own home elsewhere.

'Now, can I get you some tea? Or, better still, a cold drink?'

'Something cold, Mum. You're a lifesaver. We're both dehydrating rapidly!'

As Mrs Johnson made her way into the house, he pulled a couple of luxurious garden chairs forward.

'You were going to tell me about the secret plans for the surgery.'

His answering laugh was deep and infectious. 'It's not the actual surgery details that are secret. We just don't want to give the locals advance warning that we are planning to site a health centre on their doorstep.

'We've been on the lookout for a suitable property for a couple of years, but they're not easy to find in this area. At the right price, anyway.'

Becky nodded. 'I hope your quest is successful. Is it actually in Begstone?'

'No, in a nearby village. It sounds ideal but I'm not too optimistic. There could be many snags we don't know about. The council are the vendors so they may restrict any change of use.'

'What's it used for at the moment?'

'A private dwelling. The chap who lived in it farms the surrounding fields. He's amalgamated two farms and gone to live in the other farmhouse, leaving Paddocks empty.'

'Paddocks?' she spluttered, the colour draining from her face. 'You mean Paddocks on the Ashford Road?'

At Marc's double take she continued recklessly, 'You can't take a house like that and knock it about to make a surgery. Have you no soul?'

His dark eyes searched her face thoughtfully, before he

muttered quietly, 'You obviously know the area better than I thought.'

Becky turned to look at him, her concern causing the colour to flood back into her cheeks. 'That house was once a second home to me. It's Victorian, but built in the Queen Anne style. It's beautiful and...'

Seeing a shadow of annoyance wipe the enthusiasm for his project from his face, Becky recognised that the impulsive nature that came with her red hair had once again allowed her to make a complete fool of herself.

Even as she spoke she regretted her outburst in defence of the house, but it was too late. She stopped and added apologetically, 'I'm sorry, Marc. I didn't mean to be rude, but it was just so unexpected. I suppose my happy memories of the house are the reason I applied for a job in this area when I decided to escape the London rat race. And why I looked out that way for my flat.'

His expression softening again, he told her, 'You know, with the right people, it's possible to alter these old places with little damage to the original structure. Was it your grandparents who lived there?'

'No, my mother's aunt and uncle. They were childless so loved having us there.' She paused, as her memories continued to flood back. Memories that she wasn't prepared to divulge. How it had been a haven from her father's abuse of her mother. How, when she'd been at Paddocks, she'd felt safe, and hadn't had to cover her ears to shut out the thwacks which had always been followed by her mother's screams.

Suddenly aware that Marc was asking more about the house, she pretended to be considering carefully what he had said earlier. 'Actually, the house isn't as big as it appears from the outside. It will need to be so enlarged that

I can't believe the character of the house won't be lost. However, I guess it's none of my business.'

'You're right, it *is* none of your business but I quite understand.' Compared to its earlier warmth, his voice was as icy cool as the home-made lemonade she was now handed.

'Thank you. This is delicious and most welcome, Mrs Johnson.'

Her host acknowledged the compliment. 'Have you always lived in this area?'

Becky shook her head. 'I'm from the Midlands but for the past few years I've been working in London. However, I did live on my uncle's and aunt's farm on the Ashford Road for nearly three years, and regularly holidayed with them when I was growing up. I've always thought I'd like to settle here.'

Clearly sensing the tension between them, and possibly having overheard the end of the conversation, his mother said, 'I hope you won't regret it. Much of this area has changed beyond recognition.'

'I've noticed.' Becky smiled but, perceiving it would be politic to completely change the subject, she asked the name of the climbing rose on the pergola.

After a brief discussion on the various plants and the difficulties in retaining the services of a gardener, Becky stood up.

'I really ought to get back and finish my unpacking. Thank you for the lemonade, Mrs Johnson.'

Her son accompanied her back to her car, but his eyes were expressionless when he said, 'I'll see you tomorrow, then.'

'You impetuous fool, Becky Groom,' she told herself as she drove away. 'Why don't you keep your big mouth shut? You've certainly done a good job of antagonising your boss even before you start work. And when he'd been so kind as well.

'Even if they could get planning permission for change of use, they'll probably decide it's not suitable and you'll have created a rumpus for nothing. Goodness knows what he thinks of you, being so rude. Not exactly an auspicious start to your new position.'

Her earlier optimistic mood had evaporated and for some reason she felt totally dejected as she returned to her lonely flat and her unpacking. She couldn't help wondering if she'd made a mistake in coming back to where she'd always been so happy in the past. If she wasn't more careful, her memories would soon become tarnished.

Getting up on Monday before her alarm went off, she arrived at the surgery in plenty of time for her eight o'clock start.

'Welcome to Sandley.' Rose, the practice manager, was unlocking the door when Becky arrived. 'You had no trouble finding accommodation?'

'No. I moved down to a flat in Begstone yesterday.'

'I must get the address from you. Is it comfortable?'

'Very, and as I'm in the attic of a three-storey house, the views are wonderful.'

'Sounds good.' She checked a rota on the wall. 'You'll be working with Jan this morning. Then you'll see how we organise the tasks. She should be in any time now. Here's her surgery lists. Mostly dressings and blood tests today, with the odd inoculation thrown in.'

Becky carried the pile of notes through and placed them on the desk, then carried out a quick orientation check on the contents of the treatment room. Having worked for an agency for the last year, an opportunity to learn the routine before being thrown in at the deep end was a bonus she hadn't expected.

She returned to the desk and took out the notes on top of the pile.

The first patient, Mr Peck, was booked in for eight-fifteen. She checked her watch. Eight-twenty. The list was already running late. A fasting blood sugar. Nothing she couldn't handle. Perhaps she ought to start. She called him through.

'Hello, Mr Peck. You're for a blood test, I see.'

'That's right. I had a check-up at work and they found sugar in my water so Dr Johnson is running a few tests. The last blood tests were inconclusive so he said I had to starve overnight before this one.'

Becky nodded and gathered the equipment she needed. She had just finished taking the blood sample when the door burst open and Jan, the senior treatment-room nurse, rushed in.

'Sorry, Mr Peck, I got held up by the traffic. Nurse Groom's done the honours, I see. All well?'

'Fine. She's got my blood. I can go now, can I?'

Jan nodded and picked up his notes. 'I see you've an appointment with Dr Johnson on Friday. He should have the result by then.' She opened the door and almost propelled him through.

'Sorry about that. I'll call the next one in while you update the records.'

'Alan. Come on through.' She turned to Becky. 'Mr Brown has a leg ulcer to be dressed.' Without a word, she hustled him onto the treatment-room chair and set about removing the old dressing.

When Becky had finished her administrative work, she smiled at him and asked, 'Is it feeling any better?'

He nodded. 'The pain's eased a lot since last week.'

'That's good. How are you feeling in yourself?'

He proceeded to give her an updated account of all his ailments, and when he left Jan smiled wryly. 'It's best not to ask. There's not the time to hear them out.'

Becky raised a surprised eyebrow, but didn't comment. The remainder of the morning was a similar hectic scramble and Becky began to feel quite sorry for the patients.

When everyone on the list had at last been seen, they broke for a cup of coffee. Becky looked again at the treatment-room list. 'They're allowed even less time with us than they have with the doctors. Are you happy about that?'

Jan shrugged. 'Not really. But, with only two of us doing surgeries, it's the best we can do. Perhaps now you're here we can spread the load a little, although we still only have one treatment room. It'll be great if we get that purpose-built health centre we've been repeatedly promised.'

'Hmm, I heard that could be out towards Begstone. Dr Johnson said they are considering a house that way.'

Jan gave a brittle laugh. 'One of many. I'm beginning to think they just like looking over old houses because there's always some reason why the site isn't suitable.'

Recognising with embarrassment that she *had* made a fuss over nothing the previous day, Becky returned to the problem of giving more time to the patients. 'Presumably the three doctors don't all hold surgeries at the same time? Couldn't we use one of their rooms occasionally?'

'I suppose Steve Howard might be amenable, but I can't see Marc or Pete Robson agreeing. They seem to require access to the information stored there at all times.'

'So do you have any treatment-room lists in the afternoon?'

'Only the ante- and postnatals and the baby clinics. Oh, yes, and the well-person.'

'Could we do some of the dressings and check-ups on free afternoons, then?'

Jan appeared startled by the suggestion. 'I suppose so, but it would mean one of the doctors having to be here as well. They don't like us seeing the patients when they're not around. Perhaps we could put it to the practice meeting tomorrow.'

As that Monday afternoon was free of clinics, Jan showed Becky the various departments of the surgery. Having introduced her to the staff, she proceeded to talk about them once they were behind the closed treatment-room door.

'You met the doctors at your interview, apart from Patsy, our trainee, didn't you? She joined us last week.'

Becky nodded. 'I was told she would be starting.'

'She's getting married at Christmas. Dr Johnson is the only one not attached. Irene says he has something going with Rose, the practice manager, but if so they're very discreet.'

'I bumped into him yesterday and he introduced me to his mother. Does he live with her?'

'No. He has his own house. In a very up-market area. He was engaged to be married, but his fiancée drowned in a sailing accident.'

'How awful!'

'That wasn't the worst of it. Marc was working, so she was sailing with his father. He was drowned as well.'

Becky was appalled. 'How—how long ago was that?'

Jan shrugged. 'Before I came here…so it must be getting on for five years now. He never speaks of her, or the accident, so neither do we. I guess he hasn't found a way of coming to terms with it yet.'

Becky's heart would have gone out to anyone who had suffered such a cruel blow, but when it was Marc Johnson and his mother it had happened to she felt a sudden painful contraction of her heart and wished she'd known the day before. It certainly explained the sadness she had seen haunting his mother's eyes, and also accounted for the remoteness she had sensed lurking beneath his surface amiability.

Jan went on to describe the foibles of the different receptionists and secretaries and then mentioned the other treatment-room nurse. 'You met Irene, didn't you? She should be in any minute now.'

Becky had to struggle to pull her attention back from the Johnsons' tragedy to what Jan was saying. 'Irene? Yes— yes, I did.'

'She'll do the evening surgery today. It's up to you whether you want to stay on for a while.'

'I've nothing to hurry home for, so I think I will. Is it another routine list?'

Jan nodded. 'It's intended for those who're at work all day, but we get all sorts. Here's Irene now. You can go through the list with her.'

Jan had left and Irene was chatting to the practice manager when Marc popped his head round the door.

'Hi. How's it going?'

His greeting suggesting she'd been forgiven for her outburst the day before, Becky smiled. 'Fine, thanks.'

But her heart sank appreciably when he continued, 'I thought you'd like to know, we've been to see Paddocks today and we think it's got possibilities.'

Was that the reason he'd come in search of her? To tell her about the visit before anyone else did? 'What did you think of the house itself?'

'I must say I agree with you. It certainly has character and the setting is surely the best part. As you said, it will need a lot of alteration to make it suitable but, having searched for so long, I don't see that we can let that stand in our way.'

'No. I can see that.' Determined not to compound her earlier mistake, she said brightly, 'I hope it all works out for you.'

'I think we're in with a chance. There's plenty of room for a car park, and an entrance to it can be made off the side road, which is another bonus. It all rests on whether we can agree terms with the council now.'

Jan's chatter having convinced her that Paddocks probably wouldn't be any more suitable than the previous houses they'd viewed, Becky felt a mixture of emotions at his news. Although they hadn't rejected the house outright, at least Marc appreciated its character. Perhaps that would prevent the worst excesses she feared taking place.

'What alterations will be necessary?' She tried hard to keep any apprehension from her voice. The last thing she wanted to do was antagonise him again.

'I think I'll leave that to the architects. But you can rest assured their remit will be to try and leave as much of the fabric of the house intact as possible, and the gardens.' He dismissed the subject of the house as if it were of no further consequence. 'Are you finding your way around OK?'

'Yes. I sat in with Jan this morning and I'm going to do the same with Irene this evening.'

'You had the afternoon off?'

Becky shook her head. 'Jan introduced me to everyone and showed me the admin. system.'

He regarded her with a look that was curiously warming. It was reminiscent of his compassion for the dog the day before. 'Don't overdo it on your first day.'

Becky laughed gently. 'Today has been a rest cure after working for the agency. I was beginning to think orientation days were a thing of the past.'

'Not here. We want everyone to feel part of a team. Which reminds me, one of my patients, Carol Dent, is booked in to see Jan this evening. I'd be interested to hear your opinion of her.'

'You mean diagnosis?'

'Not really—more how she's coping. She complains of breathlessness and giddiness, but exhaustive tests have revealed nothing abnormal. I thought she might benefit from a chat away from her home environment. I discovered her daughter is paying a flying visit, so it seemed the ideal opportunity. She can't chicken out with the excuse that her husband can't be left.'

'He's an invalid?'

Marc nodded but tempered his assertion by wafting a raised hand from side to side. 'Sort of. Simon Dent has multiple sclerosis, but is in remission. She believes that if she wraps him in cotton wool he won't have a recurrence. She's smothering him with loving care when he wants to make the most of this time when he's feeling so much better.'

'Difficult…'

'Very, for them both, and I think that difficulty is probably the cause of her symptoms. But see what you think.'

Becky was tempted to point out that if the consultation was as rushed as the morning ones had been, it would be a near impossibility, but decided it wasn't the time to say so.

Once the evening list was under way, she was pleased she hadn't. Irene seemed to give as much time as was necessary to every one of her patients.

Carol Dent was the last one in. Becky watched and listened in silence while Irene tried to persuade her that her husband was capable of fending for himself at the present time.

Although she wasn't in a position to say anything about Simon Dent, Becky noticed Carol breathing far too rapidly whenever Irene suggested he could manage to do something alone.

She tried to reinforce what Irene was saying, then asked, 'Have you joined the local MS group?'

Carol shook her head vehemently. 'We don't want to see how bad he's going to get.'

'You can't know that. There's no way of predicting the course of the disease in any individual. Meeting others with MS will show you how many are able to lead self-sufficient and productive lives. You'll be amazed at what some of them achieve.'

Carol looked doubtful. 'I don't think Simon will want to join.'

'Why don't we try and arrange for an official of the local group to come and see you both at home? That way you'd find out more about it without committing yourselves.'

Carol murmured hesitantly, 'I suppose we could give it a try.'

Irene briskly pulled the desk diary towards her before Carol could change her mind. 'Tell me which days are best for you and I'll try and get that organised now.'

Becky gently continued the discussion with Carol until her colleague came back with the news that the visit was arranged.

When their patient finally took her leave, she seemed perceptibly brighter.

'Thanks for suggesting the MS group.' Irene was hurriedly clearing away the evening's notes. 'If you hadn't, we could have been here all night. Not an easy situation to deal with and one I could have done without this evening.' She locked the treatment room and made for the exit. 'We've friends staying and I said I'd be back before this.'

Marc had just finished his own surgery, and as Becky was about to follow her he called her into his room. 'That's if you can spare a few moments. What did you think of Carol Dent?'

'I got the impression that at the moment she needs him more than he needs her. She hyperventilated at any suggestion he could manage without her for a few hours.'

'I've noticed that. I think she can't cope without someone to care for. Since I've known her she's nursed both her terminally ill father and mother at home, and that whilst coping with a teenage daughter. Now they've died and her daughter's left home, she wants Simon to need her.'

'I suggested they join the local MS group so that she can see how much other sufferers manage to achieve.'

'Did she agree?'

'So-so. Irene seized the opportunity and arranged for the chairman to visit them at home.'

'You do realise that Carol will probably find many more people there who need her?'

'That can't be bad if it means her symptoms disappear,' she muttered.

He laughed at her defensiveness. 'I quite agree, and if he has a relapse they won't have to look far to find advice from others in the same situation. And if the worst scenario should happen, and he has difficulty getting about, they'll know, from others who've done it, how to adapt their transport and living arrangements.'

'I certainly hope so.'

'Talking about house alterations…'

'Were we?'

'Well, loosely.' He paused, before continuing tentatively, 'I did wonder if, before any plans are made and alterations put in hand, you'd like to visit Paddocks?' His eyes searched her face as he spoke. 'Then perhaps I can reassure you that none of us are intent on destroying its character, especially without consultation with interested parties. To that end I'd like to hear your views. How long is it since you've seen the house?'

'It must be nine years since Mum's uncle retired,' Becky calculated. 'But you don't have to do this. As long as the plans are sympathetic, I don't see any problem.'

His hesitation was fleeting, but in her heightened state of awareness Becky noticed it, together with the frown that flitted across his brow.

'A lot can happen in that time. Even now, the house may not be as you remember it.'

Becky suspected he was trying to tell her something, or at least that he couldn't guarantee the plans would be acceptable to her.

'How about a trip down there tomorrow after work? Then we could get a bite to eat.'

Unsure if the meal would be a good idea, Becky was cautious. 'I'd like to see the house, certainly.'

'I'll pick you up at half six, then. I'll let the agent know in the morning. You'd better go home now. It's been a long day. I'll see you tomorrow.' He didn't raise his eyes to meet hers again, but took out a bunch of keys and started locking the drawers of his desk.

Feeling dismissed, Becky guessed he was indicating not to read too much into the invitation. 'Goodnight, then. And thanks.'

The next morning Jan left Becky to cope with the list on her own, and although the time passed rapidly in a flurry of patients and paperwork she found she was able to find a few extra minutes for those who needed it. One such was an extra on the list, Laura Hull, who had been for a private health check which had included mammography.

She had received a letter that morning, recalling her. She

was thirty-eight and panic stricken. 'My daughter isn't two yet,' she sobbed as she entered the room. 'I won't see her grow up—perhaps not even starting school.'

Becky guided her to a seat and sat down beside her, a box of tissues in front of them. 'Getting in such a state won't help either you or your daughter, you know. This recall doesn't mean you have a problem, and certainly not that you have cancer.

'It could be for one of several reasons. The machine wasn't working properly, the radiographer had a bad day and didn't get the films quite right, or just that there's something on the film they want to take a closer look at. That's not unusual by any means. It doesn't necessarily mean you have anything to worry about.'

Her patient grasped at the hope she offered. 'You're not just saying that?' Her words ended in a hiccough as she tried to control her tears.

'Believe me, Laura, if they thought you had a sinister lump, they wouldn't waste time calling you back for another film—you'd be referred immediately to a specialist clinic.'

'You really mean that?'

'I certainly do,' Becky reassured her, while hoping fervently that the system was the same in this part of Kent as it had been in London.

Laura was silent as she digested the information, but didn't appear inclined to move.

'Where's your little girl this morning?'

'Anna? I left her with a neighbour. I didn't want to upset her.'

'Good idea. When is your recall appointment?'

'This afternoon.'

'Will your neighbour babysit again?'

'Andrew should be back from his business trip by then.

I wish he'd been there this morning. I didn't know which way to turn.'

Becky nodded. 'We're all conditioned to fear the big C, but, you know, it's not the killer it used to be. Improved treatments are being developed all the time, so even if it is diagnosed it's no longer a death sentence.'

Laura gave her a wan smile and rose from her chair. 'I'm being foolish, aren't I?'

'Not at all. Despite what I know, I'd be just the same if it happened to me. Now, why don't we arrange a time for you to pop in and see me after you've been screened? Then we can deal with any worries you may have.'

'You're very kind. I—I'd like that.'

When Becky had a free moment at the end of her list, she read back through Laura's file and gloomily discovered that Laura had suffered depression following the death of her mother from breast cancer. Why hadn't Laura mentioned there was a family history of the disease? It must have been at the back of her mind. That was why she'd been so distressed.

She closed the file with a sigh and went in search of refreshment to sustain her through the practice meeting that was due to start.

Marc was already pouring hot water onto coffee granules for himself and did the same for Becky. 'Difficult morning?' he asked, as he handed her a cup of coffee.

'Mostly straightforward, but there is one of your patients that's giving me cause for concern.'

He frowned. 'Who's that?'

'Laura Hull.'

'Come through to my room and tell me about it.' He closed the door behind them and motioned Becky to a seat.

'She had a recall letter following a routine mammo. She was in a distressed state.'

Marc responded anxiously, 'She doesn't need that.'

'I reassured her for the moment, but there was something about her that worried me so I read through her file.'

He nodded. 'You're going to tell me about her mother—'

'Yes. I wish I'd had a chance to read her notes before I saw her.'

He shook his head. 'Just as well you didn't. Laura was adopted.'

'You mean…'

'The family history in the notes doesn't apply, thank goodness. Laura's life hasn't been easy. Anna is an IVF baby.'

'I noticed that.'

'She's been through so much over the years, including the traumatic death of her adopted mother, that she finds it difficult to accept that something won't happen to destroy the idyll she and Andrew, her husband, have created. When she got that recall she probably thought it was what she feared most.'

'I can imagine.'

'Have you arranged to see her again?'

'I asked her to pop in later, after her repeat screen, to let me know what happens.'

Marc nodded. 'Well done. That means I can contrive to be around without her thinking there's some urgent reason for me to see her.'

Becky felt encouraged, not only by his words of praise but by his willingness to deal with any problems before they assumed gigantic proportions. Despite her worry at the interview that some of his ideas might be too idealistic, it now seemed his thinking was on very similar lines to her own. It was a thought that made her heart lurch with pleasure as the telephone gave its peremptory summons.

CHAPTER TWO

MARC replaced the receiver without replying to the caller. 'The others are waiting to start the practice meeting and are wondering what we're up to.'

Although they'd only been discussing work, Becky felt colour rise in her cheeks at his words, a flush that was added to as she met a battery of speculative eyes watching them enter the room together.

'Sorry for the delay.' Marc pulled a chair forward for her. 'I think you've all met Becky, apart from Patsy.'

The attractive brunette seated in the corner smiled a welcome as Marc took the seat opposite Becky and opened his file of papers.

When discussion of administrative matters had been exhausted, Marc moved the meeting on to the patients.

'Has anyone a particular problem they want to share?'

Irene mentioned Simon and Carol Dent and it was clear that most of those present knew of their problems.

'Becky managed to persuade her to meet up with someone from the MS group. The local chairman is calling on them this evening.'

'Fantastic!' Jan's exclamation was greeted with general agreement.

Marc explained. 'I should think we've all tried to persuade them to join at some time or other, so you must have great powers of persuasion, Becky.'

Conscious of his dark eyes on her as he spoke, Becky demurred. 'I don't think it was anything I did. I just happened to be the one to suggest it at the right time for Carol—she's clearly exhausted her own resources.'

'Even so, it was a master stroke to suggest someone visit them at home first,' Irene told her. 'I'm not sure they would have agreed to go to a meeting first off.'

'We'll all be interested to see how they get on.' Marc closed the subject, before saying, 'Any other problems?'

Steve Howard brought forward for discussion a couple of patients he was worried about and then Jan mentioned Becky's idea of seeing patients in the afternoon or occasionally using one of the doctors' rooms as a treatment room.

'On the days the rooms aren't needed, of course.'

As she'd predicted, Pete and Marc thought there could be problems with either suggestion. 'Especially once Patsy starts seeing patients on her own, our consulting rooms won't be free all that often.'

They talked round the problem for a few minutes and promised to give the matter some thought, but Becky wasn't hopeful.

'Perhaps the matter will be solved for us,' Marc told them. 'As most of you know, we've seen a house this week that we think could be ideal for our new premises. If we can speed up negotiations, that would be the best solution of all.'

'Does it need much alteration?' one of the secretaries asked.

'I'm afraid so.'

'So, will there be any problem with the locals?'

'You'd better ask Becky. She knows the house and the area well, I believe.'

As attention switched to Becky, she protested, 'It *was* over nine years ago. There've probably been lots of changes in the meantime.'

'You're probably right,' Marc agreed. 'Anyway, I'll keep you all briefed at our weekly meetings. If there's nothing else today, I think we're all ready for lunch.'

The meeting broke up soon afterwards amid excited chatter at the prospect of a purpose-designed health centre.

'Quick lunch, then it'll be time to brave the antenatals,' Jan murmured to Becky.

'With which doctor?'

'Marc. He's great with the mums. I'll show you the ropes and you can assist him this afternoon. Pregnant mums are not my forte.'

Later, when she joined him in the clinic, Becky saw what Jan had meant. It was the first time she'd seen Marc in action and she was impressed, as clearly were the mums-to-be.

He appeared to know instinctively the different approach needed for each of them, and though she saw a wide variation in his bedside manner that afternoon it was clear he really cared about all the mothers and the babies they were carrying.

Yet his every action was carried out with an air of detachment. As if, Becky thought, he was afraid to allow his emotions to become involved. Which, she supposed, wasn't surprising. If his fiancée hadn't drowned, he would probably have a family of his own by now.

'All straightforward today, thank goodness,' he told her as the final patient left. 'Apart, of course, from Sandra Trewitt. I wonder why she missed her appointment.'

He picked up her file. 'Thirty-four weeks. Perhaps one of us ought to go and see her.'

'Would you have been told if she'd gone into labour?'

'I should have been, but...' he shrugged '...mistakes do happen.'

'Would you like me to call on her?'

'I'll try ringing her first. But thanks for the offer.' He frowned as he made for the door. 'Unless you'd rather...'

'Not at all. I think it's better for you to ring. She's never met me.'

He was back very quickly. 'Grab your coat, Becky. Sandra Trewitt needs us. Her midwife's tied up at the moment.'

As she climbed into the passenger seat of his dark green Volvo estate, she asked, 'What's the problem?'

He didn't answer until they were under way. 'She's complaining of quite severe backache—too bad to make the journey to the clinic today. She attributes it to the decorating they were doing yesterday, but I want to check for myself. If it's a sign of preterm labour, we need to know sooner rather than later.'

He pulled the car to a stop outside a neat terraced house. They could hear Sandra lumbering to the door at his knock, and when she opened it he introduced Becky.

'Hi. I feel a fraud, bringing you out like this. It was awful when I got up this morning but it's gradually getting easier.'

Marc nodded and, after asking a few questions, carefully examined her with Becky's help. When he'd finished and listened to the baby's heartbeat, he gave Sandra a reassuring pat on the shoulder.

'I'm pleased to say it appears to be nothing more than simple backache. Probably, as you said, made worse by the decorating. Don't worry about Junior, though. The baby sounds fine.'

Sandra laughed. 'I can believe it. I think it must be a boy and he's practising for the world cup team!'

'An aching back is quite common at this stage, Sandra. Keep your back straight as much as possible and do keep to flat shoes, won't you?'

She grimaced. 'I've worn nothing else for months.'

'What about your mattress?' Marc asked. 'You need to sleep on the firmest one in the house.'

Sandra laughed. 'There's no contest! We only have the one bed, but luckily it's a firm one.'

'No more decorating for a few days, then,' Mark ordered with mock severity, 'and we'll make your visits to the clinic weekly from now on.'

His patient nodded as Becky helped her back onto her feet. 'I'll keep in touch with you over the next few days and if you want anything at all I can be reached at the surgery.'

As he had another visit to do, they left soon afterwards. 'A good idea of yours to keep in touch. From her description I wouldn't be surprised if she had experienced a touch of preterm labour earlier, but if so it's stopped now. I'll have a word with her midwife, but I think *we* must stay in contact as well.'

Becky nodded. 'I'll keep you up to date. Talking of that, I do hope we're back in time to see Laura Hull.'

Marc groaned, 'I'd forgotten about her calling. If we've missed her, perhaps you could visit on your way home.'

'I'll certainly do that. But didn't you want to see her?'

'If she's around, but I don't want to make an issue of it.'

They parked in the health-centre car park as Laura was climbing from her car. Noting the set of Laura's features, Becky smiled and led her to the treatment room.

Closing the door behind them, she asked quietly, 'How did it go?'

The girl burst into tears. 'They said everything's all right.'

Becky already had her arm around Laura's shoulder. 'That's great news.'

Laura shook her head. 'There's something they're not telling me. I know it.'

Taken aback, Becky held her at arm's length and asked, 'Why?'

'I overheard them say so, and that they would be writing to the GP about whatever it was.'

There was a loud knock on the door at that moment and Marc popped his head round it. 'Just to say I'm off and I'll pick you up—' He didn't finish his sentence but came in, closing the door behind him.

'Problems?'

Becky quickly filled him in on the details, as if they hadn't discussed Laura earlier.

'Are you sure about what you overheard?'

Laura compressed her lips to try and stem her sobs. 'Quite sure.'

He checked his watch. 'It's too late to raise the screening clinic tonight, but first thing tomorrow I'll be in touch with them and find out the truth.' He went on to reassure her that if they said everything was all right, he could guarantee everything *was* all right.

It took over half an hour of their combined patience to convince Laura there was nothing more to be done until the morning, and that in Marc's view there was nothing at all to worry about.

'I'll tell you what, though. We'll make an appointment for you *and Andrew* to see me in the morning and hopefully we can put an end to this matter there and then.'

When Laura had left, he shook his head wearily. 'I don't know how we are ever going to convince her. I've got to dash now, but I've made a note of your address so I'll pick you up later. OK?'

She nodded, and felt a faint stirring of excitement that was at odds with the purpose of their visit!

Irene was already there for the evening surgery so, having finished for the day, Becky sped back to her digs for a leisurely bath and changed into her favourite dress of turquoise silk. Marc arrived promptly, dressed casually in flecked light grey trousers and an open-necked pink shirt. Becky wondered if she had made too much of an effort to dress up until she saw his jacket and tie on a hanger in the car.

'It won't take us long to reach Paddocks. The worst of the traffic should have cleared by now. I expect you remember this road, don't you?'

'Ye-es,' Becky answered hesitantly. 'It's the road we used to come along, but an awful lot of trees have disappeared and houses mushroomed in their place. If I'd been set down on the road with no signs I wouldn't have had a clue where I was.'

'That's the problem round here. We're not far enough from London to avoid being a country suburb and so the price of property is rocketing. Are you thinking of buying a house?'

'I had intended to but, having seen the prices, I'm having second thoughts.

'If I hear of anything reasonable, I'll let you know.' Entering Marbury village, Marc turned the car slowly into the Ashford Road. 'Well, there it is ahead. Has this part changed?'

Becky looked around her slowly and shook her head. She could feel the familiar childhood excitement rising as they approached the farm entrance. Marc stopped the car and she leapt out to open the gate. He drove in slowly and parked between the rows of apple trees that made up the front orchards. Climbing back into the car she turned to him with shining eyes and said, 'It's exactly as I remember it, Marc. Neither the farm nor the house have been altered as far as I can see. I can't believe it. After all the other changes I've seen, I was dreading what I'd find.'

He stopped the car by the front door, but when he turned to Becky she was disappointed to find his face impassive.

She wanted him to share her excitement but, of course, that wasn't possible when he had seen the house for the first time only the day before. It was a thought that panicked her. If he had no feeling for the place there was no knowing what alterations he might agree to. She must somehow infect him with her enthusiasm.

Even as she sought for the words to do so, she saw him grimace. 'What is it, Marc?'

'I was just wondering if it was a good idea, my bringing you here tonight.' He tapped the steering wheel absently as he spoke.

Becky gasped with surprise. 'Why?'

'Well, now you've seen that everything is unchanged, if we buy the property and start altering it, I'm going to be the villain of the piece.'

'As long as the alterations are within reason, I won't object.' Her excitement was dampened by his brooding attitude.

'Won't you? I wonder.' Sighing, Marc opened the driver's door and climbed out. 'Anyway, let's go and have a look round.'

As Becky took the key he handed her, she was startled by their hands touching, and she didn't know whether that touch was the cause of a small quiver of excitement churning her stomach, or whether it was the thought of revisiting the one place where she'd really known happiness.

She turned it slowly in the lock and pushed the heavy door open. Stepping into the hall, she looked up to where the sweeping staircase divided on the bend and felt only disappointment. The empty house was dark and dusty and lacked the warmth and vitality bestowed on it by her great-uncle and aunt.

Perhaps Marc was right. Perhaps they shouldn't have come. It was depressing, seeing the house in this state.

Opening the left-hand door into the dining room, Becky began to feel better. The old open fireplace was still just as she remembered it. With a little bit of polish and elbow grease, the copper hood would shine as brightly as it had always done.

'Isn't that a fantastic fireplace, Marc? We used to have a log fire when we had family meals in this room. It would be criminal to remove such a treasure.'

Marc nodded, but said nothing. Watching him straighten up after peering up the enormous chimney, Becky noted with amusement the arrogant stance he unconsciously adopted, his legs straddled as if warming his rear at a non-existent fire.

She found it easy to visualise him as the handsome lord of the manor in jodhpurs and riding boots, waiting for servants to obey his every command. Her fantasy was shattered by the knowledge that he was working out how best the room could be used in the future.

Crossing to the other side of the room, Becky pulled open the door into the kitchen. It, too, hadn't changed. Nothing had been modernised, not even the old stone sink under the window.

'Even I agree this place needs something done to it. No one could be expected to prepare and cook meals here in this day and age.' Becky laughed, hoping to jolt Marc out of the morose state the house seemed to have cast on him, but he just nodded his head in agreement and opened the door into the breakfast room.

Becky's enthusiasm getting the better of her, despite all her resolve, she said breathlessly, 'Isn't this a super room?'

Marc walked to the breakfast-room window, before answering with a puzzled frown, 'As I said yesterday, you don't have to convince me of its character, but I'm amazed by your vivid memories of the place. How old *were* you when you lived here?'

'I suppose I was about seven. It was just so different from what I'd been used to.' And how, she added silently, unwilling to burden him with her childhood problems.

'Take a look at those outbuildings, Becky. I should think the small cottage across the yard would make our trainees a super home.'

'That was a tied cottage for a farm worker.'

'Well, it certainly has superb views down the slope over the fruit trees. I wouldn't mind living there myself!'

Becky looked round the breakfast room again, remembering the Welsh dresser that had stood against the wall. The early morning sun had made the dishes displayed on it sparkle. She had to blink back tears at the memory. To hide them, she crossed quickly back to the kitchen and across the large back hall to the room that had served her uncle as an office and her aunt as a utility room.

Marc looked around the stone-flagged area and then back into the kitchen. 'What do you think of the state of these?' He was already opening the door to a dusty back staircase which looked far from safe.

'Those stairs were always out of bounds to us—my uncle said they were dangerous.' Becky leaned past Marc to look up the stairwell. 'They certainly are steep. Did you try them when you came round the house yesterday?'

'Yes, they're sound enough but, as you say, steep. And very, very dirty. In fact, I think with that dress on you'd better go up the main staircase by the front door. Come on, we'll leave this for another day.'

Becky walked through the lounge, conscious of Marc

watching her savour every memory. When she stopped and gazed into the fireplace, he took her arm gently and said, 'Penny for them?'

'I was thinking of Christmases past. We had some fabulous family get-togethers.' She shivered, remembering the first parties she'd ever known. 'My aunt and uncle were so fun-loving. So full of life. It was another world—'

'You're cold,' he broke in abruptly. 'Let's look upstairs quickly and then go and find something to eat.'

Becky followed him slowly out of the room, wondering if it was her description of her family that had upset him. Certainly, something had. Perhaps it had brought back memories for him as well, but unhappy ones.

She looked for the grandfather clock to be standing in its usual place at the bend of the staircase, but she was disappointed, as she'd known she would be. It had been sold by auction many years previously. Her uncle hadn't wanted to part with it, but there had been no way it would have fitted into the bungalow.

After a quick tour of the first floor, Marc made for the stairs to go down again.

'What about the attics, Marc?' Becky stopped by the back stairs which continued on up.

'I warn you, climb those stairs at your peril in that dress. You'll come out filthy.'

'You'll be using the attic rooms?' Becky persisted.

'As offices. The house wouldn't be a viable proposition otherwise.' He took hold of her arm. 'But let's leave the details to the architects. I'm hungry. What about you?' Marc had seen enough of the house for the time being and Becky realised, having seen it through his eyes, she felt the same.

Although disappointed that he was opting out of describing any definite plans, she replied, 'I must admit it does seem a long time since my sandwich.'

Marc opened the heavy front door and, locking it behind them, said, 'I thought we'd drive a little way into the country. I know a pub that does very good meals. Is that all right?'

'Sounds great.'

Becky found the old-world atmosphere of the Plough enchanting after the brash London pubs she was used to. As she sampled the home-made steak and kidney pie, she had to agree that the meal had been worth waiting for.

Neither having room for a dessert, Marc ordered coffee for them both. Examining his profile as he addressed the waitress, Becky felt her heart lurch as she recognised just what a good-looking man he was.

'Why so thoughtful, Becky? Is it about Paddocks?'

Thankful that his probing brown eyes had not been able to read her thoughts, Becky replied hastily, 'Not altogether. I was wondering how you knew about this pub. Hearsay?'

'It has a good reputation, yes, but I bring Mother here occasionally to save her cooking. I find it difficult to spend enough time with her, so I usually try to join her for Sunday lunch.' His eyes clouded over, something she'd noticed happen more than once in the past couple of days, which confirmed Jan's opinion that he hadn't totally come to terms with the loss of his father and fiancée.

Experiencing another pang of compassion for the mother and son so cruelly deprived of their loved ones, she guessed that the accident must have drawn them closer together. Even so, she found it refreshing that he didn't mind admitting it. She'd obviously been in London too long and become cynical!

'How long have you been looking for a new site for the health centre?'

'Three or four years now, I suppose.'

'So, if all goes smoothly, you'll go ahead with your plans despite any objections?'

He turned to her with surprise. 'Things are never black and white, Becky. We'll do our best at conservation, but surely it's better the building is used, even if it is in this way?'

Her heart sinking at his unbending response, she shrugged. 'Perhaps. But I do wonder if I'll feel able to stay and work in it or if my memories will be too strong.'

He gave her a long and meaningful look. 'Once the alterations and extensions are in place, I think you'll feel differently. And I'll try to make sure that you are one of the first to see the plans.'

'But will you be prepared to alter them if I disapprove?' she teased gently.

'That I can't promise. The experts usually know best.'

She nodded thoughtfully, wondering if she was the cause of Marc losing his easygoing manner whenever Paddocks was mentioned.

When they had both drunk as much coffee as they could manage, he crossed to the bar to settle up. It was nearly eleven when he dropped her outside her flat.

'Thank you for showing me the house, Marc, and thank you for the meal. I really enjoyed the evening.'

'Good. We must do it again some time. See you tomorrow.' With a wave of his arm Marc drove off, leaving Becky surprised and pleased but at the same time just a little disappointed that he appeared to be keeping her at arm's length.

Used to the shallow relationships she'd experienced in London, she'd thought he might expect at least a goodnight kiss in return for the outing, if not something more.

Not that she was looking for anything more. The way

her father had treated her mother had made her wary when past boyfriends had wanted to move their relationships on. She preferred to keep them platonic. So far she hadn't regretted her stance.

As she got ready for bed. she wondered if the tragedy Marc had suffered had resulted in him also deciding to pursue a solitary existence, if indeed he was. Hadn't Jan mentioned a suspected liaison with the practice manager? If she was right, it didn't seem to be making him very happy.

Thoughts of him whirled round and round in her head that night, and by the morning she knew that for the first time in her life it wouldn't take much for her to lose her heart, which was foolhardy in the extreme.

'You look as if you spent the night on the tiles,' Rose greeted her the next morning. 'Everything OK?'

'Yes. I didn't sleep very well, that's all. Not used to the bed yet, I suppose.' She laughed Rose's concern away, aware that she was the last person Becky would want to know the real reason.

'I've just taken a call from Jan. She's going to be late, so could you start the list?'

'No problem. Jan's OK, is she?'

Rose hesitated. 'I guess she hasn't said anything to you, but you're going to have to know. She and her husband have been trying for a baby for some long time and she's now under the care of the university infertility team. They don't seem to give her much notice of appointments.'

'Poor Jan. No wonder she doesn't enjoy the antenatals.'

'She's very good about them, but if she can get out of the clinic she will. Understandably.'

'Do you know what stage they're at?'

Rose shook her head. 'She never talks about it. I expect Marc does, but he wouldn't break her confidentiality.'

'Of course.'

She was halfway through the morning list of patients when Jan arrived.

'Any problems?' she asked Becky.

'None at all. How about you? Everything OK?'

'Fine. I'll carry on from here. I saw Marc as I came in and he wants to see you. He's got Laura and Andrew Hull with him.'

Wondering what Marc had found out about Laura's screening, she tapped on his door and opened it.

'Come in, Becky.'

She looked towards Laura and was pleased to see how much happier she looked. 'It's all been one horrendous false alarm,' she told Becky. 'They weren't talking about me at all yesterday. Serves me right for eavesdropping.'

'I'm so glad, Laura.'

'Andrew and I want to thank you for your support. Marc's coming for dinner tomorrow night and we'd love you to join us.'

Becky looked from one to another with bewilderment as she wondered whose idea it had been that she join them and whether Marc was happy with the idea. 'Well, I…er…'

'I can pick you up, Becky,' he told her. 'It's on the way.'

Presuming that was his way of letting her know it was all right to accept, she murmured, 'That's very kind of you, then. I'd love to come.'

As Andrew and Laura rose to go, she opened the door for them.

'We'll see you tomorrow.'

When they'd gone, she turned to Marc with a suspiciously raised eyebrow. 'Is this just their way of saying thanks, or is there more to the invitation than meets the eye?'

'They want another child and have already broached the

subject with the infertility team. Laura thought this was the end of her plans and so she appreciated your sympathetic handling. If she needs to come to us for injections or blood tests, I think she'll find it easier to see you than Jan.'

'Because she's undergoing the same thing?'

Marc was hesitant. 'You know, then?'

'Rose told me this morning when Jan was late.'

He didn't respond immediately, and Becky felt he was searching for words that wouldn't break his patient's confidentiality. 'It was fine the first time around as they were both at a similar stage, but now Laura has had one child it won't be as easy.'

'I can appreciate that, but they didn't need to ask me to dinner!'

'Laura heard me say I'd pick you up last night and she put two and two together. They think they are doing us a favour. Don't worry about it.'

Easier said than done, thought Becky as she made her way back to the treatment room. Especially when Marc seemed to see no problem with it.

Jan seemed pleased to see her. 'Make us a quick cuppa, Becky. We've nearly finished the list. What did Marc want?'

'It was just that I saw Laura yesterday when she was upset and she wanted to thank me for the time I spent with her.' Becky knew she was blustering and hoped Jan wouldn't guess there was more to it than that because the last thing Becky wanted was to become the focus of speculation about Marc's private life.

It was for that very reason she had made up her mind to keep the details of the previous night's outing to herself. She'd already received evidence of the health-centre grapevine from Jan.

Becky and Jan were enjoying their lunchtime sandwich

and coffee when Rose joined them. Marc strode in a moment later.

'Everything all right, Marc?'

He nodded and seated himself beside Becky as Jan remembered she had to make a telephone call. Rose rushed across to the kettle to make him a cup of coffee, which he accepted gratefully.

'I need this. I've a horrific list of calls to catch up on.'

'Would you like me to see if any of the others can take some of them on?' Rose flashed him an appealing smile and their eyes met momentarily.

Feeling distinctly in the way, Becky was sure that the colour was flooding into her cheeks and bent to concentrate on her sandwiches, wishing there was some way she could escape.

It was a relief when Jan stuck her head round the door. 'When you've finished, Becky, I'd like your input.'

She leapt to her feet, but as she walked down the corridor she clearly heard Rose ask Marc, 'Are you coming to eat tomorrow evening as usual?'

Holding her breath, Becky paused, wanting to hear his reply. 'Afraid not. Laura and Andrew Hull have invited Becky and me for a meal.'

'I see.' Rose's tone was icy as he hurried on to say, 'Laura's been a bit upset this week and between us Becky and I sorted things out for her.'

'That's nice.' Hearing the icicles drip from Rose's voice, Becky made her way into the treatment room, more than thankful that she *hadn't* mentioned their meal at the Plough.

Jan looked up from the order form she was completing and asked, 'Everything all right?'

Becky nodded then, shrugging, she changed her mind and told Jan about the conversation she had just overheard.

Jan nodded. 'And you hadn't intended saying anything about it?'

Becky shook her head. 'I thought it would probably be politic not to.'

'Easier said than done in this environment. This place is a hotbed of gossip.'

'I guessed it would be and I didn't want to be included in it in my first week.'

Jan raised her eyebrows warningly. 'I think you might have made a mistake. It's better to be open about things. Rose is not the person to get on the wrong side of if you want an easy life. If Irene is right and she looks on Marc as her own property, she probably believes you're hiding something from her.'

Becky sighed. 'I wish they hadn't asked me. I just couldn't refuse. Ah, well, back to the grindstone. What was it you wanted help with?'

'I'm doing the monthly order, and as a new broom from London I thought you might have some suggestions for more up-to-date dressings and equipment.'

'There were a couple of things and I did notice some of the stocks are quite low.'

'I know,' Jan smiled. 'I seem to have got further and further behind with the administration recently. Now you've joined us, I'm hoping to remedy that.'

It was over an hour later when Becky remembered Sandra Trewitt. 'I must ring her,' she told Jan. 'I promised I'd keep in touch. She didn't turn up at the clinic yesterday because she had backache so we did a home visit. Marc was happy not to see her until next week, as long as he knows all's well.'

Before she left that evening, he came in search of her. 'Have you a moment, Becky? I wondered if you'd contacted Sandra Trewitt?'

She nodded. 'She's fine.'

'That's good.' He seemed distracted. 'There's something I should tell you, Becky.'

'What's that?'

'I mentioned our dinner invitation tomorrow to Rose.'

'And?'

He appeared uneasy. 'It might cause you a problem.'

'I don't see why it should,' she told him airily, 'but I'm quite happy if you'd like to take Rose tomorrow, instead of me.'

'I doubt if Laura would be happy about that.' He fixed her with a look of such intensity that for a moment Becky was overwhelmed by his masculinity.

She had seated herself in the one chair, as she now realised, where she was unable to evade his scrutiny. But when she tried to discover if he was as aware as she was of a sudden tension surging between them she was prevented from doing so by his half-closed eyelids.

She felt her pulse racing and the colour flood into her cheeks as she prayed for an interruption.

Her prayers were answered, but when it was Rose who walked through the doorway she guessed it was some cruel practical joke the gods were playing.

CHAPTER THREE

'IT'S probably best if I pick you up on my way to the Hull residence this evening.'

Becky glanced at her watch. Four o'clock. Was Marc leaving already? Of course. It was Thursday. His day to finish early.

'That sounds good. But don't rush. I'm nowhere near through here.'

'Irene'll be in soon to take over, won't she?'

Jan hadn't felt up to facing work that morning, which had left Becky to cope for the first time on her own. Not that she minded, but she hadn't been helped by Rose's total non-cooperation.

'Maybe, but she'll have enough on her own list without me adding to her load.'

'Who's left to see?' He lifted the well-person clinic list and wrinkled his nose dismissively. 'Those four shouldn't take long. All young and healthy upwardly mobiles, judging by their ages and addresses.'

'Hopefully, but it doesn't always work that way. Some of them are so far from family and friends and they have all kinds of worries. This is their one opportunity to discuss them.'

He shrugged his agreement. 'OK, then. I'll leave you to get on. Pick you up about seven?'

She nodded.

As Marc had predicted, the first three consultations were straightforward. The fourth, a newcomer to the area, wasn't.

After she had taken down his own health history, and what little he knew of his family's, and had dragged the dates of his various immunisations from him, as if she were extracting top-secret information, he sat forward in his chair and, his face the colour of beetroot, stammered in a confidential whisper, 'I—I think I—I caught something from a girl I slept with last year.'

'What makes you think that, Ryan?' she asked gently.

He ran his index finger along his groin. 'I've got a rash.'

Becky was puzzled. 'How long did you say it was since you slept with the girl?'

'Just over a year.'

'Did you use a condom?'

He nodded and clearly pathetically hopeful that Becky was going to tell him there was no problem, added, 'It was the first time for both of us.'

'You're sure of that?'

He nodded violently. 'It wasn't very pleasant. That's why we've never bothered again.'

Trying to hide her incredulity at such innocence in this day and age, Becky sought confirmation. 'You're still seeing the girl then?'

He nodded again.

'Has she had any problems?'

'I don't think so.'

'When did you first notice the rash?'

'Last month some time.'

Aware that his answers didn't point to a conclusive diagnosis, she asked tentatively, 'Would you let me take a look at the rash? Or would you rather I made an appointment for you with one of the male doctors?'

'I'd much rather you—doctors scare me.' Puzzled by his lack of confidence, she pulled the curtains that screened the examination couch.

He lowered his trousers barely sufficiently for her to see the very top of the rash, but it was enough to decide her. Becky indicated he should pull them up again.

'Have you had any problems with your feet recently?'

He nodded. 'Only athlete's foot.'

'I thought you might have. Do you do your own washing?'

Ryan nodded. 'And you wash your socks and underpants together?'

'That's right.'

'On a low temperature wash?'

He nodded again.

'I don't think you've got anything worse than a spread of your athlete's foot. It can happen. You need to see the doctor to confirm the diagnosis and prescribe treatment, but I honestly don't think you've anything to worry about.'

The relief that spread across his face at her words would have been comic if it hadn't been so pitiable.

'If you call at the reception desk, you can make an appointment. You are registered with Dr Johnson, but any of them will see you.'

He nodded.

Remembering his fear of doctors, Becky urged, 'Do it now, or you'll forget.'

'I will. I didn't want to see the doctor because I thought I might be making a fuss over nothing, but it's all right now you've told me I'm not.'

When he'd left, Becky checked again his age on his notes. Nineteen. What a sheltered upbringing he must have had. She flicked through his notes to see if there was any reason doctors should frighten him and was surprised to see that he was brought up by one—but one of a different generation. His grandfather. She read right through his notes then but there was no mention of what had happened to his parents.

After quickly tidying up and handing over the treatment room to Irene, Becky stopped at the reception desk on the way out. 'Did Ryan Green make an appointment?'

Tanya nodded.

'Do you remember with which doctor?'

The receptionist looked worried. 'Dr Johnson. That's all right, isn't it? He is his patient.'

'That's fine,' Becky reassured her. 'When's he seeing him?'

'Tomorrow. He's the first appointment. There was a cancellation.'

'Here are his notes, then. One less set for you to search out.'

Tanya took the notes gratefully. 'Thanks.'

Becky made her way out to her car as quickly as she could, hoping she wouldn't be delayed too long in the rush-hour traffic. She wanted to be ready when Marc arrived to pick her up.

She managed with time to spare, even though she wasted precious minutes before deciding on the black skirt and Chinese silk blouse with the mandarin collar.

When she opened the door to him, Marc whistled. 'Very nice. If I didn't know better I'd say you'd had all afternoon to get ready.'

'Chance would be a fine thing,' she quipped as they made their way to his Volvo.

Once the car was under way, she asked, 'Do you mind if we discuss work for a moment?'

He turned to her with a wry smile. 'If we must. That's the only problem with socialising with colleagues.'

'I need to fill you in with the details of your first appointment tomorrow. But as long as you don't start seeing patients until I arrive, we can forget it for now.'

'Oh, no, we can't. You've whetted my appetite.'

She laughed. 'It's not that interesting. Just one of your new patients who must be one of the original innocents abroad. He was worried about STD but I'm pretty sure it's nothing more than a spread of athlete's foot to his groin. He only allowed me a tiny peek, but what was strange was that he preferred to drop his trousers for me, rather than risk you telling him he was wasting your time. He said he was scared of doctors.'

'Perhaps he's had a bad experience in the past.'

'I did wonder if it stemmed from his childhood. He was brought up by his grandfather, a doctor!'

'Hmm. Sounds interesting. I'll see what I can dig out tomorrow. He's lucky to get an appointment in the morning, though.'

'It was a cancellation. At least he won't have to worry about it for too long.'

Laura's thank-you dinner was superb—avocado and prawns followed by a roast rack of lamb and rounded off with a raspberry *crème brûlée*.

It was Becky's first social engagement since her move and she couldn't have enjoyed it more.

Marc and Andrew were clearly friends, who played the odd game of squash together, and Laura made Becky feel that she belonged.

Anna had been asleep when they'd arrived, but Laura was delighted when she awoke soon after they finished their meal. It meant she could show her off. Becky took her in her arms and duly admired her. It wasn't difficult. She was one of the most cherubic babies she ever seen. And she'd seen a few in her time.

Her attention focussed on the baby she was cradling,

Becky didn't notice that all conversation had ceased until she suddenly looked up and found all three of them watching her intently.

'Looks like you're well used to babies.' Andrew smiled.

Becky glanced up at him. 'I've done quite a lot of paediatric work.'

'Perhaps it's time you had one of your own, then. Eh, Marc?'

Colour flooded into her cheeks as Laura came to her rescue. 'Shall we see if she'll settle now? Don't want to make a rod for our own backs, do we?'

Becky handed the slumbering bundle over. 'I'll come up with you.'

Once Anna was settled, Laura followed Becky out onto the landing. 'I'm sorry about Andrew's big mouth. He embarrassed you then, didn't he?'

Giving thanks for Laura's female intuition, Becky nodded. 'Marc and I are colleagues. Nothing more. I only started at the health centre on Monday and—'

'But—but,' Laura interrupted. 'I distinctly heard him arrange to pick you up on Tuesday. I couldn't wait to tell Andrew. We were delighted. Marc's been such a recluse since the accident. Work's all he's been interested in.' She clapped a hand over her mouth. 'You did know about that, didn't you?'

Becky smiled and nodded. 'Yes, I knew, but I'm afraid Tuesday was work for Marc as well. You see, I used to visit relatives in a house that he was thinking of buying to convert into a new health centre.'

'Come into the bedroom and tell me all about it.'

Becky did as she suggested. 'So, you see, Tuesday was all about gaining my support for the project.'

'And did he?' Laura queried eagerly. 'I mean, are you going to support him?'

Becky shrugged. 'As far as I can, but I'm not sure about continuing with the practice once the move is made—'

Clearly aghast, Laura broke in, 'You can't do that to Marc. I haven't seen him so happy in a long time.'

Surprised by her outburst, Becky smiled. 'Don't worry about it. It might not happen, and even if it does it won't happen overnight.'

'I hope not, because the way Marc was looking at you earlier…'

Becky laughed. 'You're as bad as Andrew, imagining things. Come on. Marc and I should have left long ago. We both have an early start tomorrow.'

Laura was reluctant to terminate their chat, but Becky was determined. Laura and Andrew were mistaken if they thought there was anything between Marc and herself, and she didn't want to encourage further speculation.

When they arrived at Becky's flat she invited Marc in for a cup of coffee.

He checked his watch and said, 'I'd love to, but it's late and we're both working tomorrow. Perhaps I could take a rain check! Maybe at a weekend when we don't have to be up early the next morning?'

She was warmly surprised by his suggestion but had to say, 'I'm not around this weekend. My friend is getting married in London and I asked for the weekend off when I was offered the job.'

He nodded. 'I remember. There'll be plenty of other weekends.'

He came round to her side of the car, and as he helped her out he kissed her on the cheek. 'I've enjoyed this evening. Thank you.'

'You shouldn't be thanking me. It was a super meal, wasn't it?'

'It was, but improved by your company,' he told her with

a morose smile that spoke volumes and twisted Becky's heart. He was clearly still grieving and, though his life was lonely, enjoying an evening out was clearly something he didn't often allow himself.

Hadn't Laura told her as much? And hadn't she said she'd not seen him so happy since the accident? Perhaps his project for the house was what he needed to bring him out of himself. If so, Becky determined she would do everything she could to help. He worked hard and cared about his patients and even after such a short acquaintance she knew she wanted him to be happy.

After a sound sleep she was optimistic about the coming day when she arrived for work, an optimism that was shattered by Rose's greeting.

'Jan won't be in again just yet so the list is all yours. And I'm afraid you'll have to do her Saturday duty tomorrow.'

'Oh, but—'

Becky started to protest, but Rose thrust a pile of notes into her arms. 'Hadn't you better get started? The first couple are here already.'

Recalling Jan saying it was a bad move to get on the wrong side of Rose, Becky shrugged and called Alan Brown through to the treatment room.

'How are you this morning?'

'Coping. I've come for my dressing, remember?'

'Of course. How's your leg felt this week?'

'It was great until yesterday. Then a lad on his tricycle veered across the pavement and ran into me.'

'Goodness, I hope you told him off.'

'He were only a tiddler, and his mother was distraught. I didn't let them know I suffered with my leg.'

Becky gently removed the dressing and cleaned the ulcer. 'I should say the accident has set the healing back

somewhat, but I don't think there's any permanent damage.
I can imagine how it must have hurt.'

'Too true, but it's easing off now.'

'How are things otherwise?' she asked as she completed
the re-dressing.

'All the better for a chat. I get quite lonely at home on
my own.'

'I'm sure you do.' Becky checked her list of appointments. 'Tell you what, there's someone else waiting now,
but if you can manage it why don't you pop back around
twelve-thirty and we can have a longer chat over a cup of
coffee?'

She watched his face light up. 'I'd like that.'

Her day was hectic and she gave up any idea of asking
Rose if it would be possible to employ an agency nurse to
cover Saturday morning.

Thank goodness she had turned down the invitation to
be the bridesmaid—her presence would have been vital
then. As it was, she would hardly be missed.

She noticed Marc coming in search of her over the lunch
hour, but when he saw she was with Alan Brown he left
her to it.

Irene arrived in good time for the hand-over, allowing
Becky to escape. She wanted to phone Teresa, the bride,
and apologise.

As she made her way towards the exit, Marc's voice
enquired, 'Busy day?'

She nodded. 'I enjoyed it, though. How—?'

She'd been about to ask about his day when he interrupted to ask, 'Are you going up to London tonight or in
the morning?'

She cast a quick glance in the direction of Reception
before saying quietly, 'I'm not going. I'm covering for Jan.'

'But you asked for this weekend off for a special reason and we agreed. Can't Irene do it?'

'It doesn't matter, Marc.' She was pretty sure that Rose had done this because Marc had cancelled his meal with her the night before in favour of herself, and to keep the peace Becky had decided to do nothing about it. 'Leave it, Marc,' she begged.

Seeing Rose leaving the premises, he ignored her plea. 'Rose. Could you give us a moment?'

Rose turned and, seeing Becky with him, nodded knowingly. 'Problem?'

'I thought you knew Becky had asked for this weekend off to go to a wedding. She can't cover for Jan.'

Rose shrugged innocently. 'She's had all day to make other arrangements. Or to ask me to do so.'

Marc frowned. 'Why didn't you say something to Rose, Becky?'

She wanted to tell him it was because Rose had made up her mind, but instead she mumbled, 'I—I just didn't find the time.'

He nodded. 'I can believe that. You didn't even stop for lunch.'

Aware he was making matters worse, Becky cringed. 'Forget it. It doesn't matter now.'

But Marc wasn't prepared to do so. 'We'll see if Irene can cover.'

Sighing with exasperation, Rose slid off her coat again and, snatching the rotas from the desk, knocked on the treatment-room door.

There was no problem. Irene could do the duty.

Rose gave them the information dispassionately and Marc went to start his evening surgery, leaving Becky feeling like a fool.

When the door had closed behind him, Rose turned to

Becky and muttered, 'What a pity you didn't say something earlier. As you see, it was easily resolved. There was no need to run to the senior partner for help.' She slung her coat around her shoulders and slammed the door as she left.

Becky went off for her weekend aware that life at the health centre was going to be even more difficult the next week.

She was right. Her hostile reception by Rose on Monday was made worse by the enjoyable weekend she'd spent with many of her old friends.

During the day, Becky made a couple of attempts to find out how Marc had got on with Ryan Green the previous Friday, but each time they were interrupted by Rose with what seemed to Becky to be spurious queries.

Becky had just completed her day's duties and was on her way out when Marc called to her. 'I believe you wanted to discuss a patient with me. I'm free now if you can spare a moment.'

He had architect's drawings sprawling across every surface in his room, including parts of the floor.

He closed the door behind her. 'I've got the outline working plans for Paddocks here,' he told her excitedly. 'I thought it'd be a good idea if you looked at them before any firm decisions are made.'

His enthusiasm was overpowering. 'Oh. I—I see,' she stammered, conscious that he had chosen a time when Rose was in Reception and had watched her through the door with an eagle eye. 'That's a kind thought, but I'm not sure I'll be any use in that direction. I just wondered how you'd got on with Ryan.'

'I'll tell you when we've had a look at these.' He indicated the profusion of drawings. 'You see, before we can go any further with the purchase, I have to apply for permission for change of use. I'm going to the planning office for a pre-application discussion tomorrow, but first I'd like a bit more background information on the village residents, and if you think they'll have any objections.'

'The Marbury villagers, Marc? That's a difficult one. They used to be a very close-knit farming community, but bear in mind I haven't been in the area for several years. In that time they've become more a suburb than a village.'

'Can you remember any of them?'

'Vaguely. Since my aunt and uncle died my mother keeps in touch with some of them.'

'I'm sure if there are any objections they'll come from the long-time residents. It's them I'm interested in. What do you think will upset them most—the increase in traffic to the house or perhaps the fact that it is no longer used as a farmhouse? I don't want to get off on the wrong foot or we could have endless trouble.'

Becky did her best to recall anything that might be helpful, but her memory was sketchy.

'Perhaps your mother would help?'

'I could ask, I suppose.' She really couldn't remember much about any of them herself and she would have expected him to realise that.

She tried to focus her attention back onto what he was saying, but they were disturbed by a peremptory knock on his door.

He looked at his watch, annoyed, and muttered, 'I'm not on duty. Steve's doing my surgery this evening so that I can concentrate on these plans.' Then he called, 'Come in.'

Becky wasn't surprised to see it was Rose.

'Problem?' Marc asked courteously.

'Not exactly a problem, but I'm leaving now and you haven't said if you're joining us later.'

'Of course.' He clapped a hand to his forehead, 'I'd forgotten. Pete wanted us to try out that new pub with him, didn't he?'

He grinned suddenly and turned to Becky. 'Why don't we all meet up there?'

One glance at Rose's grim face told her that would be a very bad idea indeed. 'I've too much to do after being away for the weekend. Another time perhaps.'

Marc seemed determined to make things worse, whether deliberately or inadvertently she couldn't decide. 'There's no way it'll be as good as the steak and kidney pie at the Plough, will it?'

She groaned inwardly at him bringing up details of the meal they'd shared the previous week. 'It might be better.'

'What steak and kidney when?' Rose wanted to know.

'Becky and I sampled its delights last Tuesday. Didn't we mention it?'

Becky glared at him, knowing that neither of them had.

Having done his worst, he grinned and changed the subject.

Later, when Becky had excused herself, Rose followed.

'Well!' she spat out the moment they were alone. 'How come you didn't let on you'd been invited out for a meal.'

'It wasn't like that.'

'You're a dark one and no mistake.'

Becky wished the floorboards would slide apart and devour her. 'You heard Marc say at the meeting on Tuesday that I knew the house they are thinking of converting. He thought I'd like to see what it's like now, before any alterations are put in hand. That's all.'

Rose sniffed suspiciously. 'How did you know the house?'

'I spent a lot of time there when I was young. Once I'd seen the house, Marc suggested the meal because it was getting so late. And he wanted to find out what I knew about the neighbours.'

'How nice and cosy.' As Rose stomped into her office, obviously thinking it was anything but, Becky seized the opportunity to gather her wits and her belongings and thankfully escape.

As she caught up with her washing and housework that evening, she wondered if there was something in Irene's theory about his relationship with Rose. If not, it seemed that Rose wanted there to be, and resented Marc discussing the plans for Paddocks with Becky.

The thought made her mind up. She *did* remember a couple of the local residents her mother had talked about a lot and still kept in touch with. She would ring home later and see what she could find out.

Despite the torrential rain, Becky got through the Tuesday morning traffic quicker than usual. Perhaps the weather had kept everyone in bed a few moments longer.

Marc came in search of her the moment she arrived.

'You're drenched as well. This should keep some of the patients away.' He closed the treatment-room door behind him.

Becky smiled her acknowledgement. 'They'll ask for a house call instead.'

'Probably. You asked about Ryan last night, Becky, and I never got a chance to answer. Your diagnosis was correct in every detail. It was his athlete's foot spreading, and it was his grandfather who had instilled the notion that he should not bother doctors with trivia.'

'Poor lad.'

He nodded. 'What was even worse was being given that cancellation.'

Becky frowned. 'Why?'

'He thought you'd asked for it because he had something serious that you hadn't told him.'

'He didn't!' Becky was aghast.

'I'm afraid he did. His grandfather doesn't seem to have done him many favours. He doesn't remember his parents. His mother died in childbirth and his father died of a broken heart a couple of years later. Luckily, he was willing to chat to me, so I've arranged to see him for a longer appointment this evening. He definitely needs help.'

She shook her head but, conscious of the time, picked the notes of her first patient off the pile.

'Er…Becky?'

'Yes?'

'Before we get stuck into another day, there's something I'd like you to know.'

'Yes?' She turned back towards him.

'I guess Rose wasn't pleased when I dropped the information about our visit to the Plough. I'm sorry if I've made the situation difficult for you.'

'It's probably best out in the open. She'd have heard about it somehow, I don't doubt.'

'Becky,' he sighed. 'I need to explain why I did it.'

'Yes?'

He hesitated, then sighed again. 'I expect you've heard about Julie, my fiancée.'

Becky nodded as he struggled to continue.

'The accident knocked me sideways. I blamed myself— still do. I really didn't care whether I lived or died.' He shuddered unhappily.

'You don't have to explain, Marc, unless it helps.'

He ignored her interruption. 'Rose picked up the pieces of my life and helped me to start putting it together again.'

He paused and drew in a lungful of air, before saying, 'Don't get me wrong. I'm very grateful to her for what she did, but a couple of years ago she split up with Tony, her husband, and has since become increasingly possessive.'

He gave a wry grimace. 'I know it's partly my fault. Initially, when he left, I didn't want to hurt her feelings by immediately cancelling our regular Thursday night arrangement when she cooked me a meal or our Monday get-togethers to try out different pubs. Usually Pete and his wife join us on those outings, so it was easy to persuade myself she wouldn't get the wrong idea.

'I realise now it's been a dreadful mistake, not only for my sake but hers as well, and I hoped, by telling her about our outing, Rose would realise that I don't sit at home, moping, when I'm not with her.'

'And did it?'

He shook his head. 'I fear not, but you see…I meet up with Tony occasionally, and although he doesn't say so I have a fair suspicion that he still loves her. I want to butt out of her life and give Tony a chance.'

Becky concentrated on watching him slide off the corner of the desk where he'd been perched, but she didn't speak.

'You do understand, don't you?'

She nodded. Oh, yes, she understood. He loved Rose but was using Becky herself as a human shield against his emotions to give Tony a fair chance. Just the kind of thing he *would* do.

'We both have patients waiting, so I mustn't keep you any longer,' he told her, 'but I wanted you to know the reason if Rose gives you a hard time.'

She nodded and said slowly, 'Thanks for putting me in the picture.' Her voice was subdued but as he pulled open the door, in an attempt to defuse the charged atmosphere she added lightly, 'My shoulders are broad. If I can be of further help, let me know.'

He turned and rested a hand heavily on her shoulder.

'Thanks for being so understanding.' He strode down the corridor to his own room to begin the morning surgery.

Becky threw a pillow across the room, then, feeling better, checked her pile of notes. Noting the name of the first patient, she almost regretted her suggestion that he leave the dressing for an extra day after the knock it had had. She called him in. 'Hello, Mr Brown. Come in and let me have a look at this leg of yours.'

As she removed the dressing, he asked, 'Everything all right, Nurse? You don't look yourself somehow.'

'I'm fine, thanks. How about you?'

He didn't digress into his usual catalogue of symptoms, but said instead, 'I saw Dr Johnson come in here and close the door. He hasn't been upsetting you, has he?'

Becky laughed. 'Of course not. He tried to update me on one of his patients last night, but we were interrupted so he made sure we wouldn't be this morning. That's all.'

Mr Brown appeared to accept her explanation. 'That's all right, then, because I'm just getting used to you. Wouldn't want you to leave.'

'No fear of that at the moment.'

Becky was surprised, but relieved, that his curiosity didn't run to asking where Jan was, and quickly completed his dressing.

'I'll see you Friday, then, if not before.' He walked stiffly to the door and Becky followed him out to call in her next patient.

Helen Adams had had a couple of moles removed from her back at the hospital and needed the sutures taken out.

'Was this a safety precaution or were they troubling you?' Becky asked as she prepared the dressing trolley.

'One was right under my bra strap and kept bleeding. The consultant thought it best to get rid of them both, especially as Dad had a malignant one on his arm.'

'How long ago was that?'

'Last year. He was lucky. The GP noticed it when he was checking Dad's blood pressure and it was removed before it had grown very much.'

'Was he a sun worshipper when he was younger?'

'He was in the RAF—worked on aircraft in Malaysia, so had a lot of sun on his arms at that time. But not since he came home.'

'He's all right now, is he?'

Helen laughed. 'He is, but we're all paranoid. I was sure I was at death's door when this one kept bleeding. I never thought about the bra irritating it.'

'Never mind,' Becky reassured her as she removed the last suture. 'Better to be safe than sorry. I expect you've been warned about the sun?'

'As I said, the whole family are paranoid. My sister and I are the original pale and interesting heroines! If there's the slightest chance of sun, I won't venture out without my large-brimmed hat. I welcome days like today.'

'Nice to hear someone's pleased that it's raining. Apart from gardeners, that is! Right, you're done now. They both look fine and are very neat.'

'Do I need to keep them dry?'

'Ignore them from now on. They'll be fine.'

'Thanks, Sister. That's great.'

As Marc had predicted, her next two patients were non-attenders and Becky seized the opportunity to make herself a welcome mug of coffee.

She'd barely started drinking it when Jan arrived. 'Hi. Sorry to have left you in the lurch. You've heard the news, I presume?'

Frowning, Becky shook her head.

'I'm pregnant, and suffering from the dreaded morning sickness! Marc says I can make it public now and I'm only to work when I feel like it.'

CHAPTER FOUR

BECKY wrapped her arms warmly around her colleague. 'That's fantastic. Congratulations. You must be over the moon.'

'Yes, well.' Jan grinned shyly. 'Marc says it's early days yet and not to get too excited. But I can't help it. And we've done it without outside help! I want to tell everyone. We've waited so long.'

Becky laughed as she led her to the nearest chair. 'Sit down before you explode. There's no one due to see us for a moment, so would you like a coffee?'

Jan nodded as Becky asked, 'How far on are you?'

'Just over seven weeks. The IVF team were waiting for my next period before starting further treatment and when I was late they soon became suspicious, but I didn't believe it until the sickness started. Even then I thought I might be imagining it.'

'I can believe that. But as Marc says, you need to take care of yourself. Good job I'm here to stand in for you. It means you don't have to worry about missing work.'

Jan nodded ruefully. 'It sounds good, but you were taken on so we could expand our services.'

Becky shrugged. 'Maybe, but we might as well wait to do much of that until we move into new premises. If all goes well, it shouldn't be long.'

'We're going for last week's house, then?'

'Yes. Marc is going to see the planning people about it this afternoon.'

'Oh, I hope I don't miss all the fun.'

Becky laughed. 'You'll be having fun of your own. But just think. If and when you come back to work we should have a treatment room each *and* a proper coffee-room.'

'Do you think we will?'

Becky said excitedly, 'I know we will. I've seen the plans.'

'Aren't you the lucky one?' a caustic voice from the corridor broke in on their conversation. 'Does that mean you won't be seeing any of the people in the waiting room until you have your new rooms? If so, I'll suggest they go elsewhere.'

Rose's uncalled-for sarcasm made Becky's cheeks burn. 'Don't be silly, Rose. There was no one waiting a moment ago.'

'Well, there is now.' She stomped off down the corridor.

Jan raised her eyebrows towards Becky. 'That meal with the Hulls has really put you on the wrong side of her.'

'It's not just that. And none of it has been through any fault of my own.' She shrugged and picked up a set of notes. '*Che sarà.* Back to work. Are you sitting in on the next consultation, Jan?'

'If you like. It'll speed things up if I complete the paperwork.'

Becky nodded and restarted her morning list. She worked fast and efficiently which meant that, with Jan's assistance, she could spend as much time on each appointment as was needed, and they still finished in plenty of time for the weekly practice meeting.

When they were all gathered together, Marc updated the members of the team about the house conversion. 'It's an ideal site for us. The best we've found by far. I'm going to the planning office this afternoon and should have more news after that.

'If the planners like the idea and the council agrees to

sell to us, there'll be a lot of work to be done, but once the decision is made I think we can move ahead quite quickly. So cross your fingers, and keep all this to yourselves at the moment. We don't want a sit-in by protesters!'

'Now, other news.' He looked round the room and his gaze settled benevolently on Jan. 'As most of you know by now, our senior treatment-room nurse is expecting her first baby. So I'd like to offer her sincere congratulations from us all.'

A blooming Jan smiled her thanks.

'She's been told by her doctor not to overdo it.' He paused for laughter as it took a few seconds for them all to remember he was her doctor. 'So I'm asking for your understanding when she doesn't feel up to an early morning start.'

There were sympathetic nods all round. It seemed her infertility problem must have been common knowledge.

'It's a wonderful stroke of luck that Becky joined us just in time to help out.' She hoped Rose hadn't noticed the conspiratorial smile he bestowed on her as he spoke, but, as she would have expected, it was a forlorn hope.

Rose opened her mouth to speak, but Marc continued quickly, 'I know she was appointed to assist in expanding the services we offer, but if no one has any objections, I'm going to suggest she is given Jan's rota and Jan can do what is needed as and when she feels up to it. Then she won't feel she's letting us down.'

Again, unanimous agreement was signified by nods from all present, apart from Rose who looked anything but pleased. 'Does that mean we're abandoning our expansion plans?' she asked querulously.

'Of course not, Rose, just delaying their implementation, either until we move to the new health centre or we have sufficient staff to do so. Or both.'

Rose accepted his reply without further comment, but Becky suspected she was far from happy about Marc making decisions without first consulting his practice manager.

Marc moved on to ask about various patients, finishing with a request for any news of Simon and Carol Dent.

It appeared no one had heard from or seen either of them since the previous week.

'That's a good sign,' Marc enthused. 'Perhaps the visit of the MS society member has done the trick. Let's hope so, anyway. Right, if that's all for today, we can break for lunch.'

Becky smiled at Jan. 'Sounds like I'm doing the antenatal clinic if I'm taking over your rota. Will you be attending?'

Her colleague laughed. 'I will, actually. But you won't! The midwives do the clinic alternate weeks. It's Emma's turn today.'

'I won't be needed?'

'Not as a chaperone, but if you've nothing else pressing, Emma would no doubt value your help. And I'm sure she'll be very happy if you get things ready for her. But what about your lunch?'

Becky tried to hide the disappointment in her voice. 'I'll take a coffee with me while I get the room ready.'

She had been looking forward to working with Marc again. Last week he had accepted it wasn't her fault that some of the notes were missing, but this week she had intended to prove her efficiency by having everything to hand.

The midwife hadn't arrived when Marc breezed in at a minute to two. 'Everything under control?'

'I think so. No midwife here as yet, but, then, there aren't any patients either. Did you have a good lunch?'

'I had a quick bite with Mum. She thinks there's something wrong with Sally and wanted my opinion.'

'Which was?'

'I think it's a combination of age and overweight. But I said I'd pop in again this evening and see if I thought a trip to the vet was necessary.'

'Oh, I do hope not.' Becky blinked back a stray tear as she thought of the tragedy they had already had to cope with. 'Your mum would miss her terribly.' She busied herself, rearranging the instruments on the trolley.

Grasping her shoulders, he swung her round and she saw amusement in the eyes that relentlessly searched her face.

'I didn't mean her demise was imminent. I'm sure the vet will be able to do something for her.'

Fire rushed into her cheeks as she realised her mistake. 'I do hope so.' She struggled to release herself. 'I think I just heard the first expectant patient arriving.'

'So did I,' he told her softly, 'but before you help Emma to get this clinic under way I just want to say thank you for caring. It's a rare trait these days.'

She swallowed hard and smiled her acknowledgement, and this time he freed her to call in the first mum on their list. It was Sandra Trewitt.

She greeted them both warmly. 'I'm getting around again. With difficulty, but I'm here.'

'How's the back?' Marc enquired.

'It was much better by Friday. I expect Nurse Groom kept you informed?'

He nodded. 'Emma isn't here yet, so I'd like to take a look at you myself.'

They chattered inconsequentially while he carried out the usual checks, then he consulted the notes as Becky helped her from the couch.

'Thirty-five weeks now, aren't you? Your dates were confirmed by ultrasound?'

Sandra nodded. 'They thought I might be a week adrift, but that's all.'

'They were probably right. I think it's unlikely you'll go to your expected date. But I might be wrong. It's a good idea to get your cases packed, though. Just in case.' He laughed at his own pun.

Sandra patted her abdomen fondly. 'The sooner the better is all I can say.'

'We'll see you next week if Junior hasn't put in an appearance by then, and when the midwife gets here, I'll let her know she might have an early call.'

Emma rushed in as Sandra left. 'Sorry I'm late but I was up most of the night and I've been behind all day.'

'Who delivered?' Marc asked.

Emma mentioned a name Becky didn't recall and so she left them to discuss the new baby while she tidied the couch for the next mum-to-be.

The remainder of the clinic was uneventful. Emma was very efficient, but she was so tired she was more than grateful for what Becky could do to help. When she was called away again as the last patient was climbing from the couch, Becky said she would clear up.

As she did so she couldn't help thinking about Marc and his mother and wondering how the dog was. He'd clearly thought her a sentimental idiot earlier, but his concern for his mother and her pet had tugged at her heartstrings.

Even though, as she had indicated to Laura the previous week, there was no budding romance.

Now where had that ridiculous thought come from? Neither of their outings of the previous week would have taken place had she not expressed an interest in Paddocks and, despite Rose's antagonism, she would be foolish to read anything more into them than that. Even if she wanted to, which she wasn't at all sure she did.

She was surprised to see Marc leaving the health centre almost immediately. 'You don't usually escape so promptly,' she joked as he cannoned into her in the corridor.

'I don't want to be late for my appointment at the planning office.'

'Of course.' She'd forgotten about that. 'I hope it goes well.'

'If there's any news, I'll let you know. Will you be in this evening?'

Unsure whether he intended to telephone or call in, she offered tentatively, 'If you haven't eaten, you're welcome to share the lasagne I have planned for this evening.'

He appeared startled by the suggestion. 'My rain check was only for a coffee! Can I let you know after I've had another look at Sally?'

'No problem.' She returned to finish tidying the treatment room. What an impetuous fool he must think her. She'd made the offer for no other reason than that she didn't think he'd have time to cook for himself, with everything else he was doing.

Yet he hadn't dismissed the invitation out of hand. Had his response meant he'd intended to call and tell her about the planning meeting over that coffee he was owed?

The thought was strangely warming as she handed over to Irene and made her way back to her flat. After a hasty clear-up, she set about making the lasagne. She put it in the fridge, intending to cook it when he arrived, and proceeded to make an accompanying salad.

She had just finished when the telephone rang—probably her mother in answer to the message she'd left on the answerphone the previous night.

'Hi, Becky.' It was Marc, and from the flatness of his tone she guessed immediately that she would be eating alone.

'Hi. No go at the planning office?'

'Oh, that. No. It went as well I could have hoped. I'll tell you about it tomorrow.' She'd been right about the lonely meal, then.

'So, what's the problem, Marc?'

'Sally. The vet has admitted her for further investigations and Mum is distraught. I can't leave her this evening.'

Hastily recovering from her disappointment, Becky murmured, 'Of course not, Marc. Is there anything I can do? You're welcome to this lasagne if it would help.'

'Mum's already pottering around the kitchen. Cooking a meal for us'll take her mind off Sally.'

'OK, then. I'll see you tomorrow. Hope it turns out to be nothing serious.'

'Thanks, Becky.' She sensed the appreciation in his voice and felt a resurgence of the warmth she'd experienced earlier. She thought she heard him chuckle, before asking, 'Dare I ask if you'll let me have another rain check?'

'I think I could allow that. Just this once, of course.'

'Thank you, ma'am. Much appreciated,' he joked. Then, more soberly, he added, 'See you tomorrow, Becky. I'll tell you about the planners then.'

She replaced the receiver and the telephone rang again almost immediately. This time it *was* her mother.

'I've been trying for ages to return your call. Who've you been talking to?'

'One of the doctors from work.'

'Hmm. You must be on friendly terms to be talking that long. What's he like?'

'Stop matchmaking, Mum. He's the practice principal and is only interested in what I can tell him about

Paddocks. They're thinking of converting it into a health centre.'

'They're not! It's a beautiful house. Perfect for a large family.' Despite her mother's reaction echoing her own when she'd first heard about the plan, Becky now defended the idea.

'You wouldn't say that if you saw it—it's empty of the warmth and vitality we both remember.' She deliberately ignored what her mother was saying at the other end of the line and added, 'Marc says they will try and keep the character of the building intact.'

'Try? That's what he would say, but it means nothing. Try! Huh,' Mrs Groom said disparagingly. 'Anyway, what did you ring me about last night?'

'Paddocks,' Becky told her innocently. 'Marc wants to know how the long-time residents would feel about it. I wondered if you would suggest who I could visit to find out.'

'I can tell you what they'll think about it. Exactly the same as I do.'

Becky was exasperated. 'You can't know that, Mum. You've never been a true resident.'

Mrs Groom sniffed. 'We lived there for a short time if you remember.'

How could she forget? 'We still weren't residents as such. Just invited guests.'

'You go and see Mrs Bennett and Miss Lewin, then. You remember them, don't you? They'll soon tell you. They both live on the opposite side of the Ashford Road. You can tell them I sent you.' Becky could hear the pages of her address book rustling. 'Number eighty, Mrs Bennett, and...er...eighty-four, Miss Lewin.'

She jotted down the numbers and changed the subject by asking how her mother was. Becky could guarantee she would have a list of health problems she wanted to discuss and Paddocks would soon be forgotten.

When she finally replaced the receiver, she contemplated visiting one or other of the ladies there and then, but, reckoning they must both be in their eighties, she decided it would be better to wait until the weekend.

Instead she cooked the lasagne, and while she ate exactly half of it she thought about Marc. And Paddocks. And Sally. And how, especially now Jan was pregnant, she was an accepted member of the health centre team. Accepted by everyone but Rose that was. She was the only one making life difficult for Becky, and unfortunately she had more opportunity than most to do so.

When her brain eventually protested at the twists and turns of her thoughts, she washed up and settled in front of the television to watch, without concentration, programmes she hadn't intended to view. Programmes that allowed her thoughts to wander again.

How could she care so much about a dog she'd met only once? She knew it was because in just ten days she had come to care about Marc more than was wise when the practice manager had staked a prior claim.

Even when she went to bed her thoughts refused to be stilled. Consequently she overslept the next morning, and arrived at the surgery *after* the first patient.

'Jan won't be in at all today and Mrs Green is waiting for you.' Rose looked at her with suspicion in her narrowed eyes, but Becky had no time to do anything more than acknowledge the information.

She swept her pile of notes off the desk and opened up the treatment room, then called her first patient. Mrs Green was for ear syringing and Becky soon carried out the task. 'That should be much better.'

'It certainly is. I feel as if you're shouting now.'

Becky laughed as she saw her out and called in the next patient.

By the time lunchtime came around she was starving. Missing breakfast had not been a good idea when she had such a heavy case load to handle. She'd had no time to make sandwiches either. She would have to find something to sustain her through the afternoon.

She quickly tidied the remnants of the morning's list and, locking the door behind her, told the young girl on the reception desk, 'I'm just popping out for half an hour. There's no one booked to see me until three.'

As she climbed into her car, she saw Marc climb from his Volvo, lugging his bulging briefcase behind him. Spotting Becky, he waved and turned his steps in her direction.

'Hi. Where are you off to?'

She mumbled with flaming cheeks, 'I overslept, so I'm going to find a pack of sandwiches.'

'Don't do that. I want to talk and we can do that without interruption over a quick snack.' He dropped his bag at her feet. 'Keep an eye on that while I check no more calls have come in for me.'

He was back within seconds and hoisted his bag aloft again. 'Lock your car. We'll go in mine.'

'Er, I told Reception I'd be back in half an hour.'

'No problem. I've told them you can be reached on my bleeper.'

Aware that was just about the worst thing he could have done, Becky raised her eyebrows and sighed deeply.

He must have read her thoughts because as he helped her into the passenger seat he said, 'If I try and talk to you in there, we're invariably interrupted.'

He swung the car out of the car park and headed towards Paddocks.

'Where are we going?'

'A place that opened recently on the outskirts of Marbury. I don't expect you'll know it.'

Becky didn't, but she was impressed by her first sight of the small bistro. Marc led her though to an orangerie at the rear. 'We should be able to talk here. It doesn't get too busy on Wednesdays.'

'It's lovely, Marc.'

'Wait till you try the food. And the service is quick. That's what I like about it.'

When they'd ordered, he leaned forward across the table. 'Sally first. The vet doesn't seem too pessimistic about her. He thinks Mum'll be able to have her home later on today.'

'That's great news,' Becky enthused, her eyes shining. 'What does he think is the problem?'

'Arthritis, old age, the odd lump and bump. No specific diagnosis as far as I could tell. As so often occurs with humans. They want something definitive but we can't give it.'

'How's your mum?'

'Delighted at the prospect of having her home again. Enough about Sally. I promised to tell you about my meeting yesterday.'

Becky nodded as their food was brought to the table. 'What happened?'

'The planners I spoke to were sympathetic about our lack of space here, but I'm not convinced they believe Paddocks is the right place.'

'Did they have any other suggestions?'

'Not really, but they said to submit our plans anyway and they'll make a decision then.'

They concentrated on their food for the next few minutes, then Marc continued, 'If they decide to sell it'll

be at a good price because it needs such extensive reno-
vation.'

'But that'll swallow up the money you would have paid,
or more, won't it?'

'Without a doubt.' He sampled another mouthful of his
broccoli bake. 'This is delicious. What I'm trying to say is
that if we're going to have to do that amount of work, at
the same time we can make Paddocks into exactly what we
want, without having to worry about cost or too drastic
alteration.'

'Ye-es, I think I see,' Becky murmured thoughtfully.

'So I want you to think about what accommodation the
expanded treatment-room services will need. And I don't
want you to skimp on anything. If you think it will be
useful, put it down.'

'Surely, as the senior, Jan should be the one to do that.'

'Jan has more than enough on her mind at the moment.
She'll be disappearing on maternity leave before we know
it and you'll be acting senior.'

'What about Irene?'

'She's great as a part-timer for the evenings, but that's
what she wants to remain. When we advertised your post,
she was invited to take it, but she prefers to remain as she
is.'

'At my interview you described how you want to expand,
but not in any detail. Before I can make any decisions I'll
need to know exactly what you all have in mind.'

He nodded eagerly. 'We need to organise a meeting with
Pete, Steve and Rose. Each of the five of us can bring our
own ideas to the table and I'm willing to bet they'll be very
similar.'

And I'm willing to bet Rose will want Jan and not me,
Becky thought as she tucked into the remains of her veg-
etable lasagne.

They were just finishing the coffee that followed their meal when Marc's bleeper went. 'Damn. Is that for you or for me, I wonder?'

He checked the number and went in search of a phone. He was back within minutes. 'Come on. We're going to deliver a baby.'

'But—but—' Becky wanted to protest she wasn't a midwife, but he didn't give her a chance.

'Sandra Trewitt's in labour and can't reach Emma. They've called an ambulance but her husband says things are getting out of hand. She's only round the corner, so there's no time to drop you back at the surgery.'

They were at Sandra's house within minutes, but not soon enough. As they rushed up to the open front door, the cry of a newborn baby greeted them. Following the sound, they found Sandra on her back on the dining-room floor and Ian, her husband, clumsily trying to wrap the baby in a towel while it was still attached to its mother.

Marc took the situation in at a glance and, grabbing what he needed from his bag, knelt beside Sandra.

'Are you OK?'

'Never felt better in my life,' she said with a beam.

He grinned and quickly checked the condition of both mother and baby, then, after pulling on gloves, proceeded to clamp and cut the umbilical cord. Becky completed the swaddling of the baby and as Ian found cushions to support his wife's shoulders and head, she handed the newborn child to Sandra to cuddle. 'Your son, if I'm not mistaken.'

Sandra lifted her son to her breast and Becky watched with fascination as he attempted to suckle at the proffered nipple.

'Great stuff, Sandra,' Marc said encouragingly. 'That should speed up delivery of the placenta.'

Marvelling at the child's instinctive response, Becky

went in search of a bowl of water and towels, then watched as a short time later the third stage of labour was completed.

As she set about making Sandra comfortable, by cleaning her up and covering her with a blanket Ian had brought downstairs, she heard with relief the ambulance siren in the distance. Sandra's regular midwife bustled in moments before the paramedics and the house was suddenly full of people.

'Well, well, what have we here?' Emma was already kneeling beside Becky and Marc and ripping open sterile packs.

He turned to her with a smile. 'Baby and placenta delivered safely. No drugs administered. Over to you now.'

Emma did all her own checking, then indicated that Sandra should be moved onto the stretcher. She turned her attention to the baby. 'Two point three kilos—just over five pounds. And you've got a fine pair of lungs, haven't you, son?'

Sandra smiled up at Ian who was holding her hand and gazing at the baby as if he still couldn't believe his part in the miracle. 'Would you mind if we call him after you, Dr Johnson?'

'Hey, steady on,' Marc protested. 'It was your husband that did all the work.'

'We don't want two Ians in the family.' Sandra chuckled. 'What's your first name, Doctor?'

'Marc,' he told her without mentioning the unusual spelling.

'That's perfect,' Sandra responded. 'Mark is Ian's second name.'

When the midwife had cleansed and swaddled young Mark again, she handed the bundle back to Sandra. After noting down everything that had been done, she gave the record card to one of the paramedics and said, 'I'll follow you to the hospital.'

Sandra's husband joined her in the ambulance after asking Marc to slam the door of the house when they all left.

Becky did her best to tidy the room while Marc and Emma discussed briefly what had happened.

'I didn't ask when her labour began, but it must have progressed pretty rapidly. I suspected she might be thirty-six rather than thirty-five weeks when I saw her yesterday but I certainly didn't expect her to rush things like this.'

'You did wonder if her backache last week was a warning, didn't you?' Emma asked.

'I did at the time, but Becky has kept in touch with her since and it all settled quite quickly. I suppose it could have started up again earlier today and she just ignored it.'

'No harm done anyway. I'll get along to the hospital now and do all that's necessary. I should imagine Baby Trewitt will be in special care for twenty-four hours after that precipitous arrival.'

Marc slammed the door behind them and was about to drive Becky back to the health centre when he must have noticed her struggling to blink back tears.

He rested a hand on her knee. 'Don't be afraid to cry. It's an incredible experience we've just witnessed, you know. Thanks for what you did.'

She sighed and wiped a stray tear from her eye. 'I felt pretty useless. I'm sure I'd have coped if you hadn't been there, but it would have been instinctive. I wouldn't have known the correct thing to do.'

'You're a practice nurse, not a midwife. And if you remain here until you retire, I doubt you'll come across another labour as rapid as that.'

Becky laughed. 'What if Sandra has another baby? Would it happen again?'

'You may not be a midwife, but you know what you're talking about. Yes, it could be even quicker next time.'

'Great for Sandra, terrifying for everyone else.'

'You can say that again.'

On their arrival back at the health centre, Rose met Becky at the door and checked her watch. 'Some half hour.'

Although Marc was a little way behind, he overheard her words and, misunderstanding her meaning, said cheerfully, 'It certainly was the quickest delivery I've ever seen.'

As Becky made her way through to the treatment room, she heard Rose enquire, 'What are you talking about, Marc?'

He frowned. 'Our special delivery, of course. Sandra Trewitt's son. He wasn't prepared to wait for the proper time and place. Emma is at the hospital with them now.'

Becky couldn't help smiling as she saw that Marc had unwittingly taken the wind from Rose's sails!

There were a couple of notes on her desk. Carol Dent had rung, wanting to talk to her, and Mr Peck had rung and wanted to talk to her about his diabetes, which Marc had diagnosed the previous Friday. He had left both his work and home telephone numbers, so she guessed it must be quite important.

She checked her appointment book and decided to tackle Carol first. 'Hi, it's Nurse Groom from the surgery. You wanted to speak to me?'

Carol hesitated, then whispered, 'I—I can't talk now.' Then she replaced the receiver.

Wondering about the best way to proceed with Carol, she decided to ring Roy Peck at work. She was more successful there. Marc had told him that diet alone would probably deal with his raised blood sugar and he had seen Irene on Friday evening.

'I'm on this diet, see. Reduced calorie. And we've been

invited to help celebrate a friend's sixtieth birthday on Friday. Can I join him in a few alcoholic drinks?'

'Well, probably not a few, but the occasional one will do you no harm, as long as you remember to take the calories it contains into account when you calculate what you're going to eat. Obviously a dry wine is better for you than a sweet one.'

There was a silence on the other end of the line.

'Is that a problem, Roy?'

'I dunno. I'm not finding it easy to keep to what it says on the sheet.'

Aware that a diabetic mini-clinic was one of the expansions shelved the previous day, Becky suggested he make an appointment to see her when they both had enough time for discussion.

'That should help,' he told her. 'When should I come?'

She checked and found the week's morning lists fully booked. 'Afternoons any good to you, Roy?'

'I could come after work, four-thirtyish.'

Becky calculated rapidly. That would give them half an hour before Irene needed the room.

She made up her mind. 'This afternoon all right?'

When he agreed and was about to ring off she reminded him, 'Don't forget to bring all your charts, then I can see how you're doing.'

The silence that preceded him replacing the receiver was ominous. Becky sighed, guessing he hadn't bothered to fill any of them in.

She wandered out into the reception area. 'Could I have Roy Peck's notes? He's coming to see me at four-thirty. And did you take the call from Carol Dent?'

'No. I did. Is there a problem?' Rose came across to the reception desk. She obviously didn't miss much of what was going on when her office door was open!

'Did she say what the problem was?'

Rose sniffed. 'Of course not or I'd have written it down. She said she wanted to talk to you, that's all.'

'OK. That's fine. Do you by any chance know how many diabetic patients we have on our lists?'

'One of our trainees did do an audit,' Rose said thoughtfully. 'If I remember rightly there were roughly ten or twelve per cent at that time. Why?'

'I was wondering if we could set up a clinic for them on Wednesday afternoons.'

Rose shrugged. 'I doubt it. The room is used every month for the baby clinic.'

'But it was free last week and this. Surely we could work out a rota.'

'You'd better ask Marc about that. It would need one of the doctors to be there and I don't think they'll be willing to add to *their* workload.'

Becky eyed Rose levelly and said quietly, 'I trained as a diabetic nurse specialist. The doctors wouldn't necessarily have to be there every time.'

Refusing to be defeated, Rose muttered, 'We'll see.' And marched smartly back into her office.

CHAPTER FIVE

WHEN Roy Peck arrived it was clear Becky had been right about him. He had neither checked his glucose levels nor recorded what he had eaten.

'Let's see how you are doing, then.' She checked his blood pressure, weight and blood sugar levels and smiled at him. 'Not bad, not bad at all, considering. You don't smoke, do you?'

He shook his head.

'And have you tried to keep to the diet even if you haven't recorded it?'

He shrugged. 'It ain't easy, but I do my best.'

'Good, because, as I'm sure Dr Johnson told you, if you can maintain reasonable control, it will drastically reduce the risks of any complications occurring. And if we can do that with diet alone, it's a big bonus for you.'

He nodded. 'I've heard a lot about what can happen to someone with diabetes from the chaps I work with, but Dr Johnson told me not to believe all I've been told. He gave me a book and a couple of pamphlets to read as well.'

'Good. The more you know about the condition, the easier you'll find it to cope. But it is important that you keep written records. We're all so busy these days that though we think we'll remember everything we don't.'

He nodded. 'I'll try. Now I can see a reason for it.'

'Right. Let's sit down together and see what you can recall about what you ate yesterday. Then you can tell me which bits of the diet you are finding difficult.'

By the time she had dealt with Roy's problems, it was

80

past Becky's finishing time, but she was still concerned about the Dents. They were Marc's patients and she knew very little about them. She needed to talk to him about them and would do so the moment he arrived to start his evening surgery.

A couple of times she knocked on his door, then she asked the receptionist if Marc was likely to be late.

'He was called away—Steve is standing in for him.'

Wondering if it was worth waiting, Becky asked, 'To an emergency?'

'Some kind of family problem,' the young girl responded vaguely, while searching for case notes to accompany the following morning's lists.

Recalling Marc saying that Sally might be home again this evening, she decided he must have gone to the vet. Which was no help to her problem with Carol Dent.

She made her way slowly back to the treatment room and when Irene was free told her about the telephone call and Carol's response. 'You know them better than I do. Would you ring again?'

'I certainly wouldn't. Carol Dent can be very touchy. She knows you've tried to return her call, so she'll probably ring back. If I hear from her this evening I'll leave you a note, but if she wants to speak especially to you I should think she'll contact you in the morning. Certainly I shouldn't worry about it. If it was important we'd have heard by now.'

Becky had to be satisfied with that, although for some reason she felt uneasy about doing nothing. On her way home to Begstone she tried to laugh off the feeling, telling herself she was allowing her imagination to run riot.

Carol had probably not wanted to ask or discuss something in front of her husband. Nothing more, nothing less.

It was ridiculous to think there was a cloak-and-dagger reason for her whispered caution.

When Becky arrived on Thursday morning it was to discover a message from Marc to say he had advised Jan to stay at home for the next couple of days.

There was no note from Irene, and as the morning wore on no telephone call from Carol Dent, so when she had a moment, Becky rang Carol's number. No reply.

She'd try again later and when Marc had finished his surgery—perhaps he'd know the best way to deal with it.

Marc, however, had left the premises by the time she had dealt with the last patient on her own list. She tried unsuccessfully to ring Carol several times throughout the day, and when she'd eventually completed her afternoon well-person clinic she went in search of Marc again but, not having an evening surgery, he had already left.

'I've not heard from Carol Dent,' she told Irene later, 'and there's been no reply all day. What do you think I should do?'

'Nothing,' Irene told her firmly. 'If there was a problem she'd have got back to you.'

Becky had to accept that Irene knew the couple and she didn't so, although she still didn't feel completely happy doing nothing, she did as suggested, resolving to mention it to Marc the next day.

Friday morning was even busier and her appointments were soon running late. Mr Brown was second on her list and couldn't be hurried. His leg was unbelievably painful and his spirits were low. When she finally managed to remove the dressing his leg ulcer looked clean and healthy, but the pain of it was clearly unbearable so she decided he ought to see Marc before the weekend.

He had no free appointments, so she asked the receptionist if she could see him before his next appointment was called.

It meant a delay to her own list, but she wasn't prepared to cause Alan Brown more pain by re-dressing the leg just so that Marc would have to repeat the process.

He rang her after only a few moments. 'Problem?' he asked tersely.

'Can I have a word?'

'If you're quick. I'm behind already.' She was surprised by his abrupt tone, but put it down to pressure of work.

She hurried along the corridor to his room and explained about the pain her patient was suffering. 'He had a knock with a kiddy's tricycle last week, which didn't help with the healing process, but it didn't appear to have done any other damage. But today the pain is obviously severe and I don't think he ought to be on his feet. He needs to be admitted to hospital for bed rest over the weekend.'

'Are you joking?' Marc snapped out the question, causing Becky to flinch inwardly, but for her patient's sake she stood her ground.

'No, I'm not. The poor man doesn't know where to put himself, the discomfort is so bad, and if he has to look after himself all weekend, I can see whoever is on call having no peace.'

'So where do you suggest we find a bed for him?'

'That I can't help you with, but I think the least you can do is see him for yourself.'

'If you insist.' He sighed and, pushing back his chair roughly, followed her across to the treatment room. His attitude was almost dismissive, something that was completely at odds with his manner towards her since she'd started at the centre. She tried to work out if she'd done something to cause him displeasure.

Puzzled by his behaviour, she could only put it down to

there being a problem with Sally and/or his mother, because under normal circumstances she didn't believe he would behave in this way. However, this wasn't the time to ask.

The moment he entered the treatment room his mood changed. His demeanour with Mr Brown was in such contrast to his bad temper that Becky could only wonder anew if she had done something to cause it.

After examining the ulcer site, he smiled and patted Alan Brown reassuringly on the shoulder. 'You *are* suffering, aren't you? And the painkillers I prescribed aren't helping?'

Mr Brown shook his head. 'I might as well eat a bag of jelly babies.'

Marc sighed. 'I think perhaps Sister is right. You need to be off your feet for a few days, but I'm not sure where we can find an empty bed. There's no one who could look after you for a short time?'

'I have a niece. In Scotland. She came down once before when I was ill. I could ask her.'

'Would you like me to talk to her?'

He nodded gratefully. 'I'll ring you with the number later.'

'How will you get home now?'

'The way I came. Shanks's pony.'

He checked the address on Mr Brown's notes. 'That trek won't help. I'll see if I can arrange a lift home for you.' He turned to Becky. 'Carry on with the same dressing and we'll visit him at home on Monday.'

He was back a moment later with some different painkillers. 'Try these over the weekend, but only these. Don't take any of the others at the same time.'

As he was about to leave the room Becky offered, 'If you don't mind waiting, I can take you home when I finish my list, but it'll be a long wait.'

Marc turned and she was acutely aware of the surprise

in the look he gave her, as if her offer had been the last thing he thought her capable of.

Unsettled, she tried to return her concentration to completing the dressing, but after seating Mr Brown comfortably in the waiting room her thoughts ran riot.

Had Marc a problem at home, or had she misread him so completely? Was the working relationship she had thought was building up between them nothing more than a figment of her imagination? Had his only interest in her been because of her knowledge of Paddocks, and now he no longer needed her input?

Desolate at the thought, she returned to her morning list and immersed herself in her work, and because she was running late she luckily didn't have another moment to allow her thoughts free rein.

It was well and truly lunchtime before she was ready to take Mr Brown home, but before she did so she tried once again to ring Carol Dent. Still no reply.

She shrugged and locked her room, before telling Tanya on Reception where she was going.

She helped Mr Brown to her car and as they drove out of the car park she asked if he needed any food for the weekend.

He shook his head. 'The home-care lady does my shopping. And cleaning.'

'So, if we organise meals for you, you could stay in bed for a few days?'

'I don't want those meals on wheels, thanks. And, anyway, I'd be bored stiff lying in bed all day. I wouldn't see a soul.'

'But if it eases the pain?'

'I'd rather suffer than be lonely, but if Fiona could come down for a few days that would be different. She's a lively soul.'

'Will you ring her yourself?'

'Aye, but I'd be glad if Dr Johnson would have a word with her as well. Just so she knows I'm not going to be a permanent burden.'

'If you give me her number, I'll see he does that this afternoon.'

When they arrived at his tiny cottage, she was pleasantly surprised. It was homely and, although the furnishings were well worn, it was spotless.

'I've lived here all my life,' he told her proudly. 'I wouldn't want to move now. Fiona wants me to live with them, but I don't want to be any trouble.'

Becky caught a nuance in his voice that was at odds with what he was saying. He was lonely and would have loved to have accepted Fiona's offer, but he was afraid. Afraid he was going to be a burden to her.

She tried to reassure him. 'I'm sure she wouldn't have made the suggestion if she had thought you'd be any trouble. It might be better for her if you moved up there. Save her worrying about you being down here on your own.'

'Mebbe.'

'Why don't you at least give it a try? Instead of asking her down here to look after you for a few days, why not accept her invitation, but with a time limit, and see how it works out?'

He looked at her with rheumy eyes. 'Do you think I should?'

'If it can be arranged, I can't see that you can lose by it.'

He nodded. 'You're like my Fiona. You really care about other people and their problems.'

Becky laughed and, thinking of Marc, said ruefully, 'Too much for my own good sometimes. But it's the way I'm made and I won't change now.' She settled him comfortably on the settee.

'I'll find you something to eat and then I must get back to the health centre to my other patients.'

She made him a light lunch before she left with his niece's telephone number. 'I'll give this to Dr Johnson and one of us will let you know what's happening. If you're going to stay here on your own, we need to find you some help.'

He nodded and was about to get up and see her out when she threatened playfully, 'Don't you dare.'

As on the previous Friday, her appointments had spilled over into a second list, and when she arrived back at the surgery the first afternoon patient was waiting.

Of Marc there was no sign, so she gave Tanya the telephone number of Mr Brown's niece and explained why he required it. 'It's important he gets it as soon as possible. Can you also tell him that I *must* see him about a patient before I leave today.'

Tanya nodded.

It was nearly four when Becky had finished her list and she breathed a sigh of relief as she switched the kettle on. If she went on missing lunch like this she'd soon lose those few extra pounds she was sure Marc Johnson disapproved of.

She was completing her paperwork when her door banged open and Marc stormed in like a whirlwind.

'Where's the telephone number Mr Brown promised me?'

Becky was so affronted by him accosting her in that way that she deliberately took her time, before spelling her answer out slowly and quietly. 'His niece, you mean? I carefully wrote it out and left it for you.'

'Where? I didn't find it on my desk.' His voice rasped with anger.

'I left it with Tanya. On Reception. I explained how important it was, and asked her to catch you the moment you put in an appearance or telephoned in. I also asked her to tell you I wanted to see you about a patient. If, as you often do, you'd just checked Reception for home-visit requests, it would have been pointless to leave my message on your desk.'

He opened his mouth to argue, but she was so incensed that she rushed on, 'And don't say you always go to your room because I've personally seen you rush into Reception to collect your messages and then leave again.'

Her disdain had the desired effect on his anger and she watched and waited as his storm abated.

At length he responded contritely. 'Tanya must have left for the weekend and not passed your message on. Do you still have the number?'

Becky took out her Filofax and, removing the page on which it was written, handed it to him. 'Apparently Fiona has asked him to move up to Scotland and live with her, but he refused.'

'Perhaps this episode will change his mind.' He turned to grasp the doorhandle.

'I suggested a limited trial run to see if they both thought it would work.'

'A good idea. Perhaps I'll say the same to Fiona.'

Sure there must have been a reason for his tetchiness that day, she decided it was an opportune moment to ask. 'Is everything all right, Marc?'

He paused momentarily, then, roughly sweeping back a straying tangle of hair, said, 'As a matter of fact, it isn't.'

'Is it Sally?'

Ignoring her concern, he ground out, 'Sally's fine.'

'So, what—?'

'You haven't heard?' he broke in. 'About Carol Dent?'

She frowned. 'No.'

'She's taken an overdose.'

Appalled, Becky whispered, 'When? How is she?'

'Hopefully, Simon found her in time, but that's not the point. Rose tells me she rang on Wednesday, asking for your help, but that you never returned the call or alerted anyone else.'

So that was the reason for his bad humour. Rose was getting her own back.

'How does Rose know I didn't return the call?' she asked quietly.

'Did you?'

'The moment we got back from delivering Sandra Trewitt's son. When I said who I was Carol said she couldn't talk and replaced the receiver.'

'And you did nothing?'

'She was your patient. I'd met Carol once and Simon never. I was going to ask your advice but you were called away and Steve did your evening surgery.'

'So you didn't bother to try again.'

Exasperated by his unwarranted accusations, Becky said icily, 'I asked Irene for her advice. She's met them both, often. She was adamant I shouldn't ring again after what Carol had said, and she said she would take the call if Carol rang back.'

'And did she?'

'No. So I have tried repeatedly over the past two days to ring her, with no success. I have also tried to meet you and discuss the matter, but you have been too busy to see me.'

She watched as the truth of what she was saying filtered slowly across his face.

'If you remember, you weren't around much yesterday. I've done all I could without actually turning up on their doorstep, and if the telephone wasn't being answered, I didn't see how that would help. The patient I wanted to see you about this evening was Carol. I'm only sorry it would have been too late.'

He ran a hand distractedly through his hair and she sensed a battle raging within him. 'It wasn't your fault,' he eventually told her quietly. 'Simon had told her he was leaving. He couldn't take her mollycoddling any longer. I should have spotted that he was desperate.'

She was instantly contrite. Sensing he was blaming himself as much if not more than her, she wanted to reassure him that it wasn't his fault either. 'You can't know everything that goes on between husband and wife.'

'Maybe not, but I knew there was a problem.'

'And dealt with it the way you thought best.'

'And we all know how often our thoughts mislead us.' His voice was so full of bitter despair that Becky was at a loss to find the right words to reassure him.

She murmured gently, 'We can only know that with hindsight, Marc.'

He shook his head vehemently. 'It's my lack of foresight that's at fault.'

'You're being too hard on yourself. You can't anticipate what every one of your patients will do.' She was only too aware how one wrong judgement or decision could cause heartache in their respective professions, but he seemed to be going way over the top.

'Unfortunately, it's not just my patients,' he told her morosely.

Realising he hadn't given her the whole explanation for his distress, she searched his face but could find no clue to what he was thinking.

'Marc—' she began.

He spoke at the same time. 'I certainly shouldn't have listened to Rose.'

She felt a sudden warmth suffuse her face as she realised he was talking about jumping to the wrong conclusion about her actions.

'Forget it,' she told him curtly, before reminding him quietly, 'Hadn't you better ring Mr Brown's niece and find out if she's willing to come down? If he's staying at home alone we need to put in some social services.' She looked at her watch. 'And that's not going to be easy at this time on a Friday.'

He sighed. 'I guess not. I'll let you know.'

Becky watched him cross to his own room with a heavy heart. Since Laura's comments about his reclusive behaviour and how much happier he'd seemed since Becky had been on the scene, she'd begun to believe that perhaps she could put some happiness back into his life. His lack of trust told her how wrong she'd been.

It was nearly time for his evening surgery when Marc found Becky alone again.

'Alan Brown's niece is coming down tomorrow to visit him and do what she can, at least for the weekend. I've been in touch with him and he assures me there's no problem this evening. He's not hungry after that sumptuous lunch you made for him.' He smiled at her for what seemed like the first time that day. 'Would that you had done the same for me. I missed lunch altogether.'

'You're not the only one,' she muttered ruefully.

Shattering any idea she might have that he was angling for an offer of hospitality, he went on to say, 'Sandra Trewitt and baby Mark are doing so well that they have gone home today. They've asked me to pop in and see my namesake after evening surgery.'

'I'm glad there were no repercussions from his unorthodox delivery.'

'Far from it. Apparently he's breast-feeding like there's no tomorrow. Sandra is clearly a natural earth mother.'

Becky nodded, but didn't respond.

'Ah! That's my first patient. I'd better go. Have a good weekend.'

Marc felt like kicking himself as he collected the notes for his evening surgery.

He had been so in tune with Becky when they'd returned to the surgery after the birth of Sandra's baby that he had even been optimistic about finding some happiness again.

News of Carol's overdose had changed that. It had revived memories he'd hoped had been consigned to the past. He should have realised that Simon had been at the end of his tether, just as he should have realised how Julie had felt about the long hours he'd been working.

He'd been trying for five years to forgive himself for that last row with her, and he'd almost succeeded. So when Rose had told him about Carol's phone call on Wednesday, he had jumped at her suggestion it was Becky's fault.

He'd been so eager not to add to his own burden of guilt that he hadn't given Becky a chance to explain.

It was no wonder she could hardly bring herself to answer him. Despite telling him to forget it, she obviously couldn't.

Having agreed to do Irene's Saturday morning clinic in payment for the previous week, Becky set out for the surgery, relieved that it was Pete Robson on call. She wasn't ready to face Marc after the disturbed night she'd spent, trying to juggle her mixed emotions and come out with an answer about her future.

She was too attracted to Marc for her to feel comfortable working with him if he didn't trust her, but until yesterday she had been so happy working at Sandley that she really didn't want to start looking for another job.

And what about Paddocks? She'd like to be on the spot to see how the conversion went. As she parked her car and made her way into the health centre, she made up her mind she would call on one or other or her mother's friends that afternoon and sound them out about the idea.

Whether it was good or bad news, she was sure Marc would be pleased to learn what they had to say.

She had plenty of time to make plans that morning as patients were few and far between. As soon as she arrived back at her flat, she searched the telephone directory for both numbers and rang Mrs Bennett first.

When her call was answered on the second ring, she was ill prepared and stuttered, 'I—I d-don't know if you remember me, Mrs Bennett. My name is Becky Groom and I used to stay with my aunt and uncle at Paddocks.'

'Rebecca?'

'That's right, but everybody calls me Becky now.'

'Is it bad news? Is it about your mother?'

Kicking herself for her thoughtlessness, Becky hastened to reassure her. 'No, no. Nothing like that. It's just that I've come to work in the area and Mum suggested I look you up. Perhaps I could pop in some time. When it's convenient.'

'How about today? Martha Lewin is coming in for afternoon tea and I'm sure she'd like to meet up with you again. We both knew you when you were knee high to a grasshopper. It'll be lovely to see you. But you'll be sad when you see Paddocks. It's been empty since your uncle left, you know, and is in a sorry state.'

She paused to take a breath, before continuing. Preferring to talk about the house face to face, Becky seized the opportunity to ask, 'What time shall I come round?'

'About three-thirty? Would that be OK?'

'Fine. Can I bring anything?'

'Bless you, no. I've done some baking already. I'll look forward to it. I don't get many visitors these days, more's the pity.'

Saddened by Mrs Bennett's obvious loneliness, Becky rounded off the call and said she would be there as arranged.

She was, however, ten minutes later arriving than she had intended as her week's shopping had taken longer than expected.

Mrs Bennett welcomed her warmly. 'Let me take your jacket.' When Becky had handed it over, she was ushered through to the living room where a sprightly Miss Lewin leapt to her feet.

'Hello, dear. Nice to see you.'

Becky offered her hand. 'And you, Miss Lewin.'

'Call me Martha, dear. You're a grown-up now and it makes me feel so old when I'm called "Miss Lewin". Come and sit by me.'

'And I'm Doris,' their host added as Becky seated herself. 'Did you take a look at Paddocks on your way in?'

Becky nodded as she accepted a tea plate and small napkin but, not wanting to broach the subject of her visit immediately, said, 'My mother asked me to give you her love. She still talks about the good times you shared in the past.'

'Aye,' Martha Lewin chipped in, 'they were good days when her aunt and uncle were at the farm. Made everyone welcome they did. Such a shame that the house isn't a home any more.'

Becky bit thoughtfully into a sandwich. 'Has it been used at all since they left?'

'Not really. I've seen lots of people traipsing round it, but no one seems to want it. I can see it soon being knocked down to make way for a housing estate. That's all they want round here. More and more little boxes.'

Becky was horrified herself at *that* thought. 'Surely the planners wouldn't allow that?'

Doris Bennett gave a brittle laugh. 'They've done it in other parts of the village. Why not here?'

Becky decided this was perhaps as good an opportunity as she was likely to get to try and find out how they would feel about a change of use instead. 'I suppose it could be used for another purpose. Like a school or—'

Martha shook her head and broke in. 'It's not big enough for a school, or offices come to that. I think that's what some of them had in mind when they came to look at the place, but it's clearly not been suitable.'

'How would you feel if someone decided it *was* suitable.'

'Anything would be better than houses. It'd be nice to at least see the place used again, rather than being left to decay.'

'I suppose so.' Becky bit into a small home-made cake. 'This is lovely, Doris. Thank you very much.'

'The pleasure's all ours. Now, tell us what your mother's up to these days. She's still living near Shrewsbury, is she?'

'She's too settled there to think of moving. She's involved with so many organisations in the village I think the place would crumble if she left!'

'That's the problem here. This is no longer a village like we remember, where we knew everyone. There's lots of commuters and not much going on. What did you say you were doing here, love? You trained as a nurse, didn't you? In London wasn't it? You did'nt go home to work near Mum, then?'

Martha Lewin seemed capable of rambling on endlessly without needing to draw a breath.

Becky nodded her agreement to all three questions. 'My friends are all in London now and although I didn't want to live in London any longer I wanted to be near enough to visit them. I'm working as a practice nurse at Sandley Health Centre.'

'They're our doctors, but it's such a distance to go when you're under the weather.'

'The practice covers a large area—it must be a problem for a lot of people without transport.' She thought about Alan Brown who walked to and from the health centre to have his leg dressed. Perhaps more home visiting by the practice nurses would be an answer.

Martha laughed. 'You can say that again. I had a taxi up the last time I went to see Dr Robson. Pity another doctor doesn't set up in opposition across the road. That's one thing Paddocks would be right for, I should think.'

Becky seized her opportunity and, wrinkling her nose, asked, 'Do you think you'd like that? It would mean cars in and out all the time. Not only during the day as it would be if it were offices, but evenings as well.'

'A bit of life across the road would be just what the doctor ordered.' Doris chuckled wickedly. 'And, just think, we'd know who was expecting an addition to the family and who was on their last legs. And how easy it would be when *we* need to see a doctor.'

'It sounds good, but I shouldn't think there are enough patients to warrant another doctor's surgery opening up, so I'm afraid you'll just have to put up with Dr Robson.'

PLAY THE FREE

"LAS VEGAS"

GAME!

HOW TO PLAY:

1. Carefully scratch off all three silver panels on the righ᷈ Then check the claim chart beneath to see how many **FRE GIFTS** you can claim.

2. When you send back this card you will receive specia᷈ selected Mills & Boon® novels from the Medical Romance series. These books have a cover price of £2.40 each ar᷈ are yours to keep, absolutely FREE.

3. And there's no catch. You're under no obligation to b᷈ anything. And you don't have to make any minimu᷈ number of purchases - not even one.

4. The fact is that thousands of readers enjoy receiving boo᷈ by post from the Reader Service™. They like th᷈ convenience of home delivery and they like getting th᷈ best new novels before they are available in the shop᷈ And of course, postage and packing is **COMPLETE᷈ FREE!**

5. We hope that after receiving your free books you'll want᷈ remain a subscriber. But the choice is yours - to contin᷈ or cancel at any time. So why not take up our invitati᷈ with no obligation of any kind - you'll be glad you did!

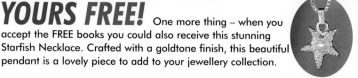

YOURS FREE!

One more thing – when you accept the FREE books you could also receive this stunning Starfish Necklace. Crafted with a goldtone finish, this beautiful pendant is a lovely piece to add to your jewellery collection.

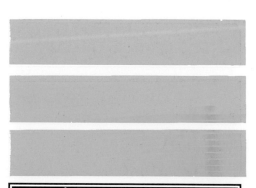

CLAIM CHART			
7	7	7	**WORTH 4 FREE** *Books plus a Necklace*
🍒	🍒	🍒	**WORTH 3 FREE** *Books plus a Necklace*
🔔	🔔	🔔	**WORTH 2 FREE** *Books*

YES! I have scratched away the three silver panels above. Please send me all the FREE gifts for which I qualify. I understand that I am under no obligation to purchase any books as explained on the opposite page and overleaf. I am over 18 years of age.

MS/MRS/MISS/MR _____ INITIALS _____ M0BI

BLOCK CAPITALS PLEASE

SURNAME _____

ADDRESS _____

_____

POSTCODE

MILLS & BOON READER SERVICE™
FREE BOOK OFFER
FREEPOST CN81
CROYDON
SURREY
CR9 3WZ

NO
STAMP
NEEDED IF
POSTED IN
THE UK
OR N.I.

'He's all right. Better the devil you know.' Martha laughed. 'And they're a good-looking bunch at Sandley. Don't you think so, Becky?'

'I've only been there a couple of weeks but they all seem very pleasant to work with.'

'That poor Dr Johnson,' Doris confided. 'His father and fiancée drowned in the same accident. Did you know that?'

'I had heard.'

'When I see him I wonder how he manages to keep going, saving other people's lives.'

Becky smiled. 'I don't suppose he thinks of his job as being quite as dramatic as that, but he does strike me as a very good doctor.'

'He'd make someone a good husband, but they do say he shuns the company of single females.'

'And who's "they"?' Becky grinned, sensing where the conversation was leading and wanting to divert it.

Doris shrugged. 'Those of us who've lived here all our lives. We meet at the shops and someone always has a tale to tell. There's not much goes on that we don't know about.'

'When you next go shopping, you can tell them about my visit and give them news of Mum.' Becky grinned to herself. That should boost their importance for a day.

She had finished her tea and found out all she needed to gauge their reaction if the health centre relocated, so she thanked both ladies and took her leave.

Pleased with her detective work, she looked forward to the forthcoming week at the health centre and to learning about the progress of Marc's plans for Paddocks at the weekly meeting. However, after Friday, she decided she wouldn't rush to inform him about the likely lack of opposition from the long-time residents.

Perhaps when he updated them on the progress at the Tuesday meeting would be a good time to mention it.

Becky was preparing for her Monday morning list when Marc wandered into the treatment room.

'Did you have a good weekend?'

Although his bad humour of Friday was no longer evident, Becky didn't feel quite ready to open up to him as she had done previously. She nodded. 'And you?'

'So-so. I spent a lot of time with Mum. Sally still isn't up to much.'

'Is she at the vet's?'

'No. That's the problem. Mum is terrified of being alone with her in case something happens. And I feel it's going to.'

Her caution forgotten, she said breathlessly, 'Oh, Marc. I'm so sorry.'

'Hey, I didn't come to burden you with my troubles, but to update you about a couple of patients. We won't need to do Alan Brown's home visit today as his niece and her husband have taken him back to Edinburgh with them.'

'Was he happy about that?'

'Delighted. Although he's always refused their invitation to live with them permanently, he fairly jumped at their offer when they came down on Saturday. My guess is he'll stay up there and before long put his cottage here on the market, but we'll have to wait and see.'

'And the other patient?' she prompted, wanting to get her surgery under way.

'Carol Dent is home and I've spent a lot of time chatting with them both this weekend.'

'And?'

'It's ironic, but I really think this episode has done them both a world of good. They're going to need a whole lot of support over the next few weeks, but I think they're beginning to understand one another better than they ever have since Simon was diagnosed.'

'That's great news, Marc. If there's anything I can do…'

'I'll remember. And now we must both get cracking with our next crop of problems. By the way, I doubt if Jan will be in very early, if at all. She's really suffering at the moment.' He spun on his heels and was gone, leaving Becky to wonder why he was telling her all these things instead of sharing them with everyone at the weekly meeting. Could it possibly mean he was trying to prove that he trusted her after all?

CHAPTER SIX

MARC returned to his consulting room, relieved to have made a start on re-establishing the rapport between them. He had spent a miserable weekend bitterly regretting his behaviour.

When Becky had arrived in Sandley she had brought a breath of fresh air into his life, and she was such a caring person that for the first time since Julie's death he had felt a re-awakening of his emotions.

She disturbed him, and he had been tempted to rush headlong into a relationship with her, but thoughts of his mother held him back. They had both been bereaved at the same time, and although he had refused to move back in with her he felt she might resent an interloper in the close relationship built around the memories of their loved ones, even though she had seemed to like Becky well enough when she had met her.

Now there was the added problem of Sally. His professional eye told him she wasn't long for this world. How would his mother cope with another loss? No. He had good reason to be cautious. He needed to move slowly if he wasn't to store up problems for any future relationships.

'Have you a moment, Marc?' He'd been so deep in his own thoughts he hadn't heard Becky approach.

He looked up and laughed. 'To be exact, three of them before my first patient is due. What can I do for you?'

'I'm sorry to bother you, but Roy Peck, the diabetic, is in my room. He didn't have an appointment but panicked when he tested his blood sugar this morning and it was practically off the scale. I thought you ought to know.'

'Not following the diet?'

'No. He came to see me last Wednesday because he isn't coping at all well and I thought I'd convinced him not to go over the top in celebrating his friend's birthday at the weekend, but apparently not.'

'Perhaps this fright will prevent a repetition.'

'Maybe, but the problem seems to be that he feels hard done by because he hasn't met anyone else struggling with a similar diet.'

Marc nodded thoughtfully. 'Would you like me to see him?'

'Not if you're happy for me to have another go at convincing him. I don't mind seeing him as and when, but I did wonder how you'd feel if I hold a diabetic mini-clinic on the Wednesdays the room is free. If we could get them chatting together about their problems, it would be a help to quite a few of them and make life easier for all of us.'

'There's no baby clinic this week, so arrange to see him then and we'll discuss the pros and cons of it at tomorrow's meeting. In the meantime, could you jot down your ideas for such a clinic?'

The suggested clinic was the first thing on Marc's agenda when they gathered together the next lunchtime. 'As you probably all know, Becky is trained as a diabetic nurse specialist and she's keen to help our diabetics by running a mini-clinic.

'This would mean regular checks for those on our lists, and an opportunity for her to engage in some group health education.'

'It would also spark off an exchange of ideas, and recipes, between the patients themselves,' Becky enthused. 'I've seen it happen before, between both the patients and their relatives, and it seems to make life easier for them all, especially as regular hospital visits will no longer be necessary. It's much better if they can be seen here at the surgery they know.'

'I think it's a brilliant idea, but when are you suggesting we hold this clinic?' Patsy asked.

'I thought of Wednesday afternoons, apart from the one when the room is used for the baby clinic—'

Rose broke in. 'It would mean one of you doctors losing a free afternoon each week.'

'Not necessarily,' Marc said. 'Becky would be able to manage alone, although I would suggest one of us putting in an appearance once a month.'

Patsy smiled. 'I'd be very interested, Becky, but you probably know more than me about the subject.'

'Why don't we start a three-month trial and then evaluate the benefits?' Pete suggested. 'If it's successful, I'm happy for you to use my room on the last Wednesday in the month.'

'I suppose if you all think it's a viable proposition, I'm over-ruled.' Rose made a note in her diary.

Becky was surprised by her reaction after her earlier antagonism to shelving their expansion.

'What objections do you have, Rose?'

'No actual objections, Marc, but I thought we'd agreed not to expand until after the move.'

'That's the general idea, but as this would use the staff and facilities already available, I think it's a special case. And while we're talking about expansion, Rose, the medical and nursing staff need to meet up with you and decide exactly what accommodation will be necessary in the future if we carry out all our plans. How about tomorrow lunchtime?'

'Will Jan be back by then?'

Becky hid a smile at Rose reacting as she had predicted.

Marc raised a warning eyebrow towards her, then turned to Rose and said, 'I'm not sure, but it won't matter. Becky will do the job just as well.'

Rose shrugged her acceptance, but Becky read the doubt in her eyes and wished there was some way she could persuade Rose that she wasn't a threat.

'Any other business today?' Marc asked.

After Rose's opposition to her last suggestion, Becky was hesitant to float her next idea, but as it had been playing on her mind since her visit to her mother's friends the previous Saturday she felt compelled to mention it.

'One other development I've thought we might be able to implement when Jan is back in harness is some limited home visiting by one or other of us.'

Marc nodded encouragingly. 'It would benefit patients like Alan Brown who live quite a distance from the surgery but who need regular dressings—'

Rose broke in, 'Surely that's the province of the community nurses?'

Having backed Becky over the diabetic clinic, Marc seemed to be playing down his support for this idea. 'It's a grey area, Rose. He's not housebound, but it would probably assist healing if he didn't have to trek up here twice a week.'

'But he'd miss the company,' Rose suggested.

'That's very true,' Becky agreed. 'I wouldn't suggest it should be a regular occurrence, only if there is an exceptional need and there are two of us on duty.'

'We do cover a large area,' Pete agreed thoughtfully, 'and the bus service isn't all that good for the far-flung patients.'

Becky couldn't resist adding, 'Apparently some of the

more elderly have to use a taxi they can ill afford to get here.'

Rose frowned. 'That shouldn't be necessary. Marc, Pete and Steve regularly visit our older patients.'

'I do know that, and I wasn't being critical, just feeling guilty at being underemployed when Jan is in.'

She made the feeble joke in an attempt to defuse Rose's hostility and Marc smiled gratefully, but Rose had the last word. 'That won't happen often. We'll need some of Irene's holiday evenings covered soon.'

To her relief the matter was dropped there, but Becky was conscious of Marc watching her, and her guilty conscience wondered if he was trying to work out who had mentioned the taxi journeys to her, and why.

Marc said there was no progress to report on Paddocks and, suspecting Rose saw her as a new broom who thought she had all the answers, Becky decided it wouldn't be a good time to mention her visit to her mother's friends.

Patsy wanted to discuss a couple of patients with the medical staff, so the reception staff left them to it.

When the meeting finally broke for lunch, Rose followed Becky along the corridor. 'I don't know how you persuaded Marc to back you about the extra clinic, but I can imagine.' She disappeared into her office and slammed her door.

Becky made herself a cup of coffee and took it into the treatment room, a cold chill spiralling down her spine. Perhaps she hadn't won the day after all.

Marc's antenatal clinic was due to start before long, so she shrugged off her pessimism and set about preparing for it.

When he came into the room before she had everything ready, he told her that he'd ask Jan to pop in and see him before the clinic proper started. 'I may not want a chaperone…'

'I understand what you're saying. I'll be in Reception if you need anything.'

As a pale-faced Jan came through the door at that moment, he pressed his hand to Becky's shoulder and whispered, 'Thanks.'

Jan smiled wanly at Becky. 'Thank goodness you're here covering for me.'

'No problem. I'll see you when you're finished with Marc.'

Becky spent the time in Reception searching for a couple of sets of notes that she hadn't been able to find earlier. When Marc called her into the treatment room, Jan was smiling.

'All's well except for not being able to face food, but Marc says I should be over the worst in a couple of weeks. I can't wait.'

'I'm keeping the treatment room warm for you, so don't rush back.'

'Marc tells me you're starting up a diabetic clinic tomorrow. Brilliant.'

'Do you have any suggestions you'd like to see incorporated in the future plans? Or any that you insist be included? We have a meeting tomorrow.'

'Nothing specific but I've given Marc my list. If I think of anything else I'll let you know. Oops.' She covered her mouth with her hand and made a dash for the loo.

Marc watched her and shook his head. 'Poor kid. It's going on all day but she doesn't want to take tablets.'

Becky moistened a clean hand towel under the cold tap. 'I should think not, after all they've been through. I'll just check if she's all right.'

When she emerged with Jan a few moments later, Marc was seated at her desk. He acknowledged Jan's hasty wave and Becky felt his eyes on her back as she tenderly ushered her friend to her car.

When she returned to start the clinic proper with him, he motioned her to the other chair. Leaning backwards until he tipped the chair slightly, he murmured, 'You do have an incredible sensitivity to the needs of every one of your patients, no matter what their age.'

His gaze was fixed on her with an intensity that disconcerted her and she tried to drag her eyes away.

'I'm a nurse. I'm trained to feel that way.'

Crashing the chair back onto its four legs, he stood up and crossed to where she sat. 'I've worked with a lot of nurses, Becky, but never one quite like you.'

Although she was more than pleased by the return of his good humour and could have listened to his compliments all afternoon, it was the wrong time when there were mums waiting to be seen. She jumped up and joked airily, 'I'm unique, that's why, and I don't think we should keep our antenatals a moment longer.'

As she crossed to the door she heard him mutter, 'There you go again, putting others first.' She ushered the first mum-to-be in with a ridiculous warmth flushing her cheeks, and was gratified to note that *his* emotions weren't totally under control.

It was something that wasn't helped for either of them by the nature of the clinic. Pregnancy might be a natural biological function, but it was surrounded by a mystical aura whose influence could be wide reaching.

More than once during the afternoon she caught Marc with a brooding expression as he listened to a foetal heartbeat, or felt a sudden movement beneath his hand. Each time, when he realised she was watching, he turned his attention to more practical matters.

There were no outstanding problems, so when the clinic

finished mid-afternoon he thanked her warmly and said, 'I'm off to see the Dents. I'll let you know how I get on.'

'Wait. You've forgotten your pen.' She held it out and as he took it she felt his fingers brush briefly against hers, startling her whole body into an unbelievable awareness.

She looked up to find his gaze fixed on her face, as if he couldn't quite believe what he had just experienced, but even as she watched, his eyes appeared to shutter against her searching gaze. Realising she was holding her breath painfully, she gasped and turned away, pretending to concentrate on the instrument trolley. When she turned again he was gone.

Marc made his way to his car unable to believe he could have been so affected by nothing more than a close encounter of their hands. Having made his decision to take things slowly, the last thing he had expected was for his body to rat on him and react to her touch with a burning awareness that he hadn't experienced since Julie died. He'd felt like a fantasising prepubescent and her reaction had made it clear that she knew it.

What must she think of him? A grown man with a professional career behaving like a gauche schoolboy. He could only put it down to the emotionally charged antenatal clinic that afternoon. Thank goodness he didn't have to return to the surgery later in the day. Perhaps by tomorrow he would have corralled his emotions into some kind of control.

Becky had intended to work late that evening, drawing up detailed plans for her diabetic clinic the next day, but as five o'clock approached she felt so emotionally exhausted that her mind refused to co-operate.

She collected together the literature she thought she would need, and after checking with Irene that she wouldn't

want any of it for the evening surgery she drove slowly
back to the flat.

She couldn't understand what the matter was with her.
She always enjoyed her work but dealing with mums-to-be
and their impending miracles had certainly got to her in a
big way that afternoon. Was it that one of their own, Jan,
was pregnant? Had her visit to the clinic made Becky conscious of her own biological clock?

Until now she hadn't given it a thought. She had been
so determined to avoid the mistake that her mother had
made that she hadn't cared that it was ticking away with
increasing speed. Suddenly she was no longer sure that she
wanted to spend the rest of her life alone. Or to miss out
on the miracle of childbirth.

Had that been the real cause of her body's reaction to
Marc that afternoon? He had certainly given her no cause
to think of him as anything more than a colleague. If she
wasn't to make a complete fool of herself, she must somehow gain control of her emotions before she met up with
him next.

Which wasn't until after she had completed her
Wednesday morning list.

'All set for this afternoon's clinic?' he asked when they
met up in the coffee-room.

'I think so, especially as Roy is the only one attending
today.'

'No, he isn't.' Patsy joined them. 'I've added a couple
to your list this morning—one insulin dependent and one
not.'

'Great. Have you got their case notes?'

'They're on my desk. Both diagnosed in the last month.'

'Either of them my patients?' Marc queried.

'No. They're both registered with Steve.'

'That's OK, then. If they'd been mine they might have

thought I was checking up on you, so you won't mind if I look in on your project this afternoon, Becky. I might learn a thing or two.'

She grinned mischievously. 'You might learn a lot—from the patients and their spouses. My experience in the clinics has taught me that living with diabetes is not as easy as most doctors seem to think.'

Marc grimaced towards Patsy. 'That's telling us both.'

'Speak for yourself. My handbook tells me my best tutor is always the patient. I think I agree.' She gave a low chuckle which made Marc and Becky laugh as Rose and the other partners joined them for their discussion on the expansion of the health centre services.

Everyone present had his or her own ideas how things should go and the discussion was both frantic and edifying. Becky left with copious notes to make sense of.

Her first diabetic clinic went well. After assessing the three patients individually, she chaired a discussion on diet which she could see was an eye-opener for Roy Peck. He stayed to listen when the chat turned to the use of insulin, and Becky watched as the realisation dawned on him that if he could maintain control with diet alone, he was the lucky one.

When he eventually left, she knew he would make a much greater effort to follow his suggested diet, and she said as much to Marc, who had been quietly observing from a corner of the room.

'I know. You could see the resolutions slotting into his mind as he stored every piece of information away. Well done, Sister Groom, diabetic supremo.'

He rested a congratulatory hand on her shoulder. 'I wonder if you'd be interested in coming to a drug company do with me tomorrow night? The lecture's on the different insulins now available and it's followed by a buffet supper.'

Another invitation, but again a plausible reason for it. She slid from under his hand and, amused at her naïvety of the previous day, smiled as she told him, 'Sounds right up my street. Thanks for asking me. I'd like to come.'

'I'll pick you up from home around seven, if that's OK? I'll be at a principals' meeting all day tomorrow, so a locum is taking my morning surgery.'

'I'll be ready.'

And she was. Just. Once again her well-person session ran way beyond its supposed finishing time. She crawled home through heavy traffic and showered so quickly that her skin was still damp under her blue glazed cotton suit when she opened the door to him.

'Hi. You look, oh, so cool and inviting to a man who's been listening to dreary lectures all day.'

Her eyes scanned the masculine elegance of his body clad in casual trousers and a leather jacket. She knew he wouldn't have worn that outfit to the meeting, so it was obvious he hadn't come straight to her flat, but she still asked, 'Would you like a drink to revive you?'

'I'd love one, but I don't think I ought to accept.'

She was about to protest, when he added, 'This bash started five minutes ago.'

During the journey, Becky asked tentatively, 'Did you see the Dents on Tuesday?'

He nodded and after a moment's thought said, 'I do intend telling you everything that's happened with Carol and Simon but not tonight—when we have more time to spare.'

Surprised, she turned to look at him but could read nothing in his expression as he watched the road ahead. Recalling how he had blamed himself for Carol's overdose, she presumed he still wasn't ready to talk about it.

She changed the subject by asking which drug company was giving the lecture they were going to. He handed her a paper containing the details of the talk and by the time she had read it they had reached their destination.

They were greeted in the hotel foyer with a glass of wine and led through to a large room where the talk had just begun. Despite the fact that it included a heavy sales pitch, Becky felt she gleaned a fair amount of useful information.

When it had finished, she turned to Marc with a smile. 'That was good. I'm glad you asked me along.'

'I've heard it before, so I knew you'd appreciate it.'

Startled, she wondered why on earth he had bothered to come to a talk he'd already heard. Was he using the meeting as another excuse to enjoy her company without commitment?

She sought for the words that might prompt him to give her a clue, but he had already turned away and was being greeted by one of the company representatives.

He turned to her. 'Phil says to follow him before all the food disappears.'

When they'd filled their plates with what Becky was surprised to find was a very substantial buffet, and found a corner to sit down, she couldn't resist voicing the thought that was uppermost in her mind. 'It was very good of you to sit through all that spiel again just for me.'

He laughed. 'You think that was why I did it? I came for the food. I'd sampled that before as well.'

She knew by the tone of his voice that he meant it as a joke, but she sensed an undercurrent of truth in his words. He almost seemed afraid that she might believe he'd come to the lecture a second time for her benefit, and she could only think it was because he felt he would be betraying Julie if he allowed himself to search for happiness again.

As they said their farewells to the sponsors of the meeting, her thoughts were elsewhere. She was wondering about the wisdom of inviting him to take up his rain check when they reached her flat, or whether, under the circumstances, she would be wiser to gently back off.

The decision was made for her. They were crossing the hotel foyer when the unexpected sound of Marc's bleeper brought them both to a standstill.

She frowned as he took it out and checked the number. 'You're not on call, are you?'

He shook his head and she could see he was worried. 'It's the Dents' number. I gave my number to Carol only to be used in the event of an emergency. They live just around the corner.' He turned to the drug rep. who had welcomed them earlier.

'Greg, you live at Begstone, don't you? Could you drop Becky home for me?'

'I don't mind coming with you,' she offered, but he shook his head.

'It's best I go alone. I'm sure you understand.'

She did, and yet she didn't, but she could do nothing but watch as he sped out of the door. She shrugged and grinned at Geoff. 'Looks like you're lumbered with me.'

He grinned. 'No problem, as long as my wife doesn't hear that I took a redhead home!' He took her arm and reassured her, 'Don't worry about it. It's no problem. Now, what's the address?'

'Difficult patient, is it?' he asked as he swung into the driver's seat of the car emblazoned with the logo of a newly merged drug giant.

'I guess so.' Becky didn't intend to continue that discussion and tried to turn the conversation to the care of diabetics. It was a subject which by that time the rep. had had more than enough of so it was a relief to them both when he pulled up outside her flat.

'Thanks for the lift, and for the evening. It was very enjoyable and informative,' she added politely.

Images of what the problem might be with Carol Dent, and how Marc was dealing with it, filled her mind well into the early hours. Perhaps he wanted to explain all at the next practice meeting rather than tell each of them individually.

He arrived late for his Friday morning surgery, and to her chagrin their paths didn't cross all morning, until she couldn't help wondering if he was avoiding her.

She crossed to the reception desk, before making herself a lunchtime coffee.

'Is Marc free, Tanya?'

'He's not in.' She looked surprised that Becky didn't know.

'Has he not been in at all?'

'Oh, yes, he saw all his patients, before rushing off to the local newspaper office.'

'What, the *Gazette*?'

'I suppose so. He's furious with them.'

'Why?'

'Haven't you seen it? They've printed a piece about our plans for the old house.'

'No! No wonder he's annoyed.'

After a quick bite of lunch, she returned to seeing her overspill list of patients, all the time keeping an eye out for Marc. He didn't return, however, until Becky was about to leave for the weekend.

'Have you just come from the newspaper office?' she asked him as he rushed in.

He frowned. 'Of course not.' His response was short. 'I've been visiting patients all afternoon.'

'Did you discover how the story reached the *Gazette*?'

His look was bleak as he said, 'They refuse to divulge their source.'

'Is—is it going to cause a problem?'

'Only time will tell.' He was clearly upset and she

thought it was probably politic to steer the conversation away from the subject.

'How did you get on at the Dents' last night?' she asked as she followed him into his consulting room.

'Fine.'

'You mean it wasn't an emergency?'

'It was, but I resolved it.'

'So, what—?'

'I've patients waiting to see me even if *you've* finished for the day.'

Aghast at his attitude, she couldn't move for a few seconds. 'What are you insinuating? This is my official finishing time.'

'That was a plain statement of fact. I wasn't accusing you of skiving off early.'

Before she could summon up a suitable response, he strode into his surgery and closed the door.

Becky stared at the closed door in disbelief. She didn't think she'd ever met anyone who could blow so hot one moment and so cold the next.

She had intended to try and alleviate his worry about the damage the article had done by telling him that he was unlikely to get opposition from the long-standing residents, but she wasn't prepared to do so while he was in that mood.

As she strode angrily out of the health centre, she gave a sudden giggle as she asked herself if there was something about Fridays that put him into these moods. If so, she'd better avoid him next week!

She spent most of Saturday and Sunday at home, catching up on her many chores, half expecting him to ring and apologise for being so abrupt with her for no reason. But her mother was the only person to telephone all weekend.

When she arrived at the health centre on Monday morning, she found Jan already in the treatment room. She looked pale and Becky was concerned about her.

'I'm much better now and feel able to cope with a morning's list, which is just as well because Marc wants one of us to join him and an architect on a visit to Paddocks.'

'What for?'

'To check their ideas for the treatment rooms. To make sure they aren't making any glaring mistakes before they finalise the plans.'

'You're the boss. You should make the final decision.'

'Please, Becky. I can't face the car journey. I'd rather stay here quietly. Anyway, as you know the house, you'll be much more use than I would be. And working for the agency, you must have seen many different surgeries. You should be full of ideas including all the latest ones. I've just stagnated here.'

'All right,' she protested laughingly. 'You can lay off the flattery now. I'll go. Did Marc say what time?'

'He'll come and find you.'

It was a typical Monday morning. Jan tried to catch up on some of her paperwork and Becky didn't have a breather between patients until way past eleven when Marc came in search of her.

'We're ready to leave, so Jan's taking over in here.' He spoke abruptly and, turning sharply on his heel, strode ahead of her to his car.

Geoff, the architect, broke the uncomfortable silence once they were under way. 'I hear you once lived in this house.'

'Yes, my great-uncle and aunt farmed there. Mum and I lived with them for a short time and I spent most of my holidays there.'

'It's going to need quite a lot of work done to it. It's been neglected for a long time. Marc tells us the dining room has to be kept more or less as it is unless it's an absolute impossibility. I gather that you were rather effusive about it.'

The smile on Geoff's face as he said this brought a flush to Becky's cheeks as she tried to imagine what Marc must have said. She was thankful that Geoff had turned his attention from her and was watching the road ahead as he chatted to Marc.

Ignoring their conversation, Becky sat quietly in the back seat and mulled over what Geoff had just been saying. She found it difficult to believe that Marc had even remembered what she had said about the dining room, never mind made that stipulation.

She decided she found Marc a very confusing person. Somehow she couldn't reconcile the Marc who had barely spoken to her since their interrupted night out with the drug company with one who had taken the trouble to ask the architects to spare the fabric of the dining room.

'Here we are.' Geoff, jumping out to open the farmhouse gate, brought Becky out of her reverie.

As he climbed back into the car she asked, 'Have you earmarked which rooms will be the treatment rooms?'

'Not exactly, because we thought the best results would probably be achieved by siting them in the extension. Then you can have exactly what mod. cons you want. What do you think of that idea?' Marc by this time had parked the car and was unlocking the front door of the house.

'It sounds as if it might be good, depending on where you intend to site the extension and whether we will be in direct contact with the reception area.' Becky hesitated while she thought of other snags that might arise.

Geoff unrolled the plans and showed Becky the provisional design.

She was surprised and pleased to see that most of her

suggestions to Marc during her second week at the surgery had been incorporated. The dining room was to be made into a plush waiting and reception area, leaving the fireplace and all the other features of the room intact.

Taking the plans with them, they went out to inspect the suggested site for the treatment rooms.

Becky could see the architects' ideas made sense, and it didn't take her long to agree with them. After further discussion on the proposed layout, Geoff rolled up the plans and said they would bring them to her for comment when they had been drawn up properly.

'Marc and I just want to go up to the attic and check a couple of things,' Geoff said as they re-entered the house. 'We won't be long as I have another appointment at twelve-thirty. If Bob arrives to pick me up, you can let him know where I am. I shouldn't come up if I were you—the stairs are filthy.'

Becky nodded her agreement and wandered into the old utility room, her mind already transported back to the past when her uncle's old roll-top desk had stood in the corner.

Gazing out of the window at the large back lawn, she recalled the many times her uncle's dog, Tim, had begged her to throw his ball just one more time. She smiled at the crab-apple tree still shedding its fruit onto the grass, providing irritating obstacles for the mower.

The sound of footsteps brought her back to the present. She glanced at her watch and, seeing it was nearly half past twelve, guessed Bob would soon be here to pick up Geoff for their next appointment. Turning, she saw Marc standing just inside the doorway.

'What—?' she began to ask, but broke off as he strode purposefully across the room towards her. Backing away at the intense look on his face, she found herself up against the wall. Looking up into a pair of blazing dark eyes.

CHAPTER SEVEN

PINNING her there by resting his hands either side of her head Marc muttered, 'Rather convenient, this. You've no patients to rush off to see, and neither have I. And there's no one to interrupt us.'

Determined not to be intimidated, she glared up at him and demanded sarcastically, 'Do you have a problem?'

'I want to know why you have made our plans for this house known to all and sundry?'

She couldn't credit he could believe she would do anything like that. Jumbled thoughts of the past, mingled with his unfair accusation, reminded her of her father regularly accusing her mother unjustly and how, when she'd been at Paddocks, there had always been someone to prevent his verbal abuse turning to physical.

She struggled to gather her thoughts and find the words that would refute his accusations once and for all.

'You are not leaving here until you tell me, so you might as well make it sooner rather than later.' When Becky still remained silent, he continued, 'I just want to know what you are playing at.'

She tried to move away, but he repositioned his hands to prevent her doing so, although she knew she could escape if she really wanted to.

'Don't be silly, Marc. What will Geoff think? He'll be down to wait for Bob in a minute. They have another appointment.'

'I know that. They are well on their way to it already. Didn't you hear Bob's car? Well? I'm waiting.'

Aware that she had been so lost in her thoughts of the past that she had heard nothing until Marc had come in search of her, Becky shuddered inwardly at the memories.

Marc looked down into her eyes and, reading the distress in them, felt an uncontrollable remorse urge him to sweep her up into his arms and make love to her until all trace of the doubt he was causing her disappeared.

Instead, he said as gently as he could, 'Whatever you've done, I have no intention of hurting you, Becky. But I need to know the truth. Rose tells me she was driving along Ashford Road last Saturday and saw you going into a house opposite Paddocks.'

'Yes. I——' Becky was about to explain her visit, but he cut her short.

'I asked that our proposals be kept quiet for the time being.'

'I'm aware of that.'

'Yet you went rushing off to tell the very residents who are going to be the most affected? I don't call that very loyal.'

'Am I going to be given a chance to explain or I am once again tried and found guilty?'

As she finished speaking he realised for the first time since he had seen that article on Friday that he could be doing her an injustice. He groaned and gave in to his earlier urge. Sweeping his arms round behind her, he gathered her into a suffocating embrace, pressing his lips gently on hers.

Caught unawares, Becky offered no immediate resistance, allowing him to press her body into contact with his. Rising fury at his behaviour soon made her body stiffen at his attempt to humiliate her. And at Paddocks of all places.

Despite her determination to get away from him, the close proximity of this man, whose charms she had tried so hard to resist, combined with the heady sweetness of his musky aftershave, affected her like expensive champagne. Becky felt sure if he let go of her now she would be unable to stand unaided. Sensing the demanding nature of his kiss, she was nevertheless surprised at his gentleness and felt herself relaxing.

Recognising the fact, Marc deepened his kiss, but as it became more probing and sensuous Becky tensed again in a furious effort to prevent herself responding. At length he lifted his lips from hers and his eyes searched her face.

'Well, now, are you going to tell me what you were doing on Saturday, or are we going to stay here all day? I've plenty of other ideas how we could spend the time.'

Furious at her body's traitorous response to his kiss, Becky dragged her eyes away from the intense depth of his scrutiny. She was searching for some way to escape from such an emotionally turbulent proximity. Only then would she be able to defend herself rationally against his accusations.

When he relaxed his hold slightly, she seized the opportunity and pushed him away from her.

'I thought I detected a response there. Just what game are you playing, Becky?'

'Game? You call this a game?' She glared up at him with venom in her eyes. 'I certainly don't. If you must know, I did sound them out on the house conversion but it was on a purely hypothetical basis. It was them who brought up the idea of using it for a doctor's surgery.'

He opened his mouth, but she held up a hand to prevent him interrupting. 'Oh, not the Sandley one. They hoped a new doctor might see its possibilities, and I don't blame them if you behave as unpredictably with your patients as you do with me.'

'Becky, I—'

She didn't let him finish. 'I'd mentioned offices, schools

and other organisations that might use the house and they dismissed those suggestions, but the idea of having a health centre on their doorstep rather than rows and rows of little boxes appealed to them.

'I humoured them, but I certainly didn't breathe a word of your plans. If someone told the *Gazette*, you'd better look elsewhere for the informant.'

'So why on earth didn't you tell me what they'd said? You knew I was worried about their reaction. I even asked for your help. So why keep it to yourself if you didn't have something to hide? You've had a whole week to do so, for heaven's sake. It's no wonder I believed what Rose was telling me.'

'Perhaps it was because I guessed you wouldn't believe I hadn't told them what you were planning,' she said quietly. 'I'd like to get back to work, please, Marc.'

She marched out of the house without looking at him. He followed and locked up, then opened the passenger door of the car for her in silence.

Attempting to ignore her still trembling reaction to his kiss, she climbed in without a word, and neither spoke throughout the short journey. He dropped her at the door of the centre and sped away again to start his visits.

Having finished her lunch, Jan was back in the treatment room. She looked up and smiled. 'Well, what do you think?'

'I'm very impressed with the plans,' Becky replied evasively.

'But?' Jan asked.

'There is no but. If it all works out to plan it'll be a super place to work.'

Jan sighed. 'Just my luck to be on maternity leave.'

'I should think that would be far preferable to the upheaval of moving all the records and equipment.'

A hint of wistfulness must unknowingly have crept into her voice because Jan picked up on it immediately. 'You need to find yourself a husband before you get too broody.'

'Broody? Me? Never.' Becky laughed. 'Well, I don't think so. It was just you and the antenatal clinic on Tuesday that made me think perhaps I was missing out. I've never felt that way before.'

'Perhaps it's the first time you've met someone you'd like to father your children,' she countered with a twinkle in her eye.

'What do you know that I don't?'

'Come off it, Becky. It's pretty common knowledge around here how you and Marc have felt about each other since the day you arrived.'

'Well it's certainly not to me,' Becky retorted heatedly.

Jan appeared unconvinced by her vehemence, but to Becky's relief, after giving her a doubting look, she must have sensed it wasn't a good time to enlarge on her suspicions and changed the subject.

It was just after three when Marc eventually returned to the surgery. Becky was busily searching for notes of some of the diabetics booked in for Wednesday and she watched relief spread across his face at the sight of her. Did he think she'd have walked out by this time and told everybody why?

A lingering trace of his aftershave reached her nostrils, transporting her thoughts momentarily back to the empty room. She turned away in case he should see her confusion.

'Have you a moment, Becky?' he asked quietly.

'I'll be through with this in about ten minutes.' Her reply was short and she didn't look at him.

Rose came out of her office and looked from one to the other wordlessly. Marc spun on his heel and left without a word.

'He doesn't look too pleased with you?'

She made the statement in the form of a question and Becky knew she would not let the matter rest until she had an explanation. She shrugged. 'We don't see eye to eye on what he's planning to do to the house.'

'Oh, I see.' Rose went back into her office, no doubt pleased that disagreement over the house had succeeded in alienating them where she had failed.

Although surprising herself at the accomplished liar she was becoming, Becky told herself it was all for the best. Rose might be a bit more pleasant to work with if she was confident that any liaison that might have developed between Marc and Becky was a thing of the past.

Becky for her part wished things could be that simple. She knew Marc had been correct when he'd said he had detected a response to his kiss. It had taken all her strength of will not to respond to him much more avidly. She was attracted to him in a way she had never experienced before, and the fervour of her response had only been restrained by her not being sure he was ready to risk commitment in case it tore his life apart again.

She knew her own emotions had been ready to surrender unconditionally when she learnt from Geoff that he cared what happened to the dining room she felt so strongly about, but she was still as confused as she had been when he'd entered the utility room with his accusation. Why had he kissed her? Did she really mean something to him, or was it some sort of sweet revenge for her supposed misdemeanour?

Becky's head began to spin as the thoughts chased one another round and round in her head. She tried to push them to the back of her mind and concentrate on what she was doing, but it wasn't easy, especially as she'd had nothing to eat or drink since her breakfast!

Marc would just have to wait until she'd remedied that. She wanted all her wits about her for *that* interview. 'OK if I put the kettle on?' she called to Jan. 'I've just remembered I haven't had any lunch. I wondered what was the matter with me.'

'Good idea.' Jan came out to join her. 'Then you can fill me in on the rest of the details of our new des. res.!'

Becky had told her earlier in the afternoon about the decision to locate their rooms in an extension, and now she explained the finer details of the layout.

They were just finishing their discussion when Marc came in search of her and snapped, 'Here you are.' Her delay had obviously done nothing to placate him.

'I needed this. I missed out on lunch.'

She hid a grin as a guilty look flashed across his face. Hunching his shoulders, he turned and left them without another word.

Having finished her tea, she arched an amused eyebrow in Jan's direction and followed him into his consulting room. He closed the door behind them.

'Sit yourself down, Becky. I'm sorry if it was my fault you missed lunch.'

She smiled sweetly. 'It'll no doubt do my waistline good.'

His glance swept down to her midriff. 'You don't need to lose any weight,' he told her gruffly.

Surprised, but pleased, she acknowledged his comment. 'I'm glad you think so. Now, what was it you wanted to see me about?'

'I want to discuss Carol Dent with you, but before I start I want to clear up a personal matter.' Becky thought she had never seen his manner so stiff and impersonal.

He continued, 'I'd like to apologise for my behaviour at

Paddocks. It was unforgivable of me to take advantage of you in that way.'

Becky was about to regretfully agree it was best forgotten when he said softly, 'I really must stop listening to Rose's tales about you.'

'She does seem to have it in for me.'

'I really am sorry I doubted you, Becky, but when her information came in conjunction with the article in the newspaper, and they refused to reveal their source, what was I to think?'

'You could have asked me…'

'But you had said nothing about visiting them. After our discussions and visit to the house, I would have expected you to let me know something so important immediately.'

'I did intend to, but…' She hesitated, not wanting to sound defensive.

Marc ignored her interruption. 'I just saw red at the thought that you, of all people, had done this, especially when I'd made a point of asking you all at the meeting to say nothing.'

Realising she wasn't completely blameless, she murmured, 'I can appreciate that, Marc. I would have told you but it was just never the right time. So, what's happening to the Dents?'

He opened a file of notes. 'Yes, well, that's another thing I need to apologise about. I thought if you couldn't be trusted with the information about the house, I certainly wasn't prepared to tell you about my chats with Carol.'

Furious, Becky leapt to her feet. 'You—you mean you doubted my confidentiality?' She sank back onto her chair and rested her head in her hands. Calling into question her integrity about the house, that was one thing, but distrusting her professional confidentiality—that was something else altogether.

He must have sensed her despair. He crossed the room in one stride and wrapped his arms around her. 'Becky, you're the last person I should doubt. I know it now and I knew it then. I can only put the fact that I did so down to a mental aberration—'

'Without trust, we can't work together,' she broke in, as if she hadn't listened to what he was saying, and freed herself from his hold. 'It'll be best if I resign with immediate effect.'

He uttered an anguished groan. 'That's the last thing you must do. I need you and so do the patients, especially Carol and Simon…'

He perched on the desk in front of her and she moved her chair back a few inches. 'You're talking nonsense now, Marc. I've never even met Simon.'

'Please, listen, Becky. You probably wondered why I didn't want you to come with me on the visit Thursday night.'

She shrugged.

'Carol was dreadfully ashamed of what she'd done and—'

He got no further because the door banged open and a wild-eyed Rose shrieked, 'Come quickly, Marc. It's Jan. She's…'

Becky didn't wait to hear more. Surely the poor girl wasn't going to lose this desperately wanted baby? Tanya pointed to the door. 'She's in the treatment room.'

Becky raced through, closely followed by Marc. Jan was seated on the examination chair, blood streaming down one side of her face.

She grinned at them both. 'Don't panic. I'm fine.' She was trying in vain to staunch the blood trickling from a cut on her right temple with a blood-soaked handkerchief.

'I'll get some dressings.' Becky was soon back with a

handful of sterile packs. She opened one for Marc who was attempting to examine the extent of the cut.

'It's not as bad as the blood loss makes it look. What on earth happened, Jan?'

'I climbed on the stool to check the tubular bandage stocks and somehow slipped off it.'

Marc checked her pulse and the reaction of her pupils. 'Did you pass out?'

'I don't think so.' Jan didn't seem as if she really remembered.

'What caused this cut?'

'Judging by the chaos, I must have hit the lower shelf as I fell.' She gestured towards the scattered needles and syringes on the floor.

'But you don't remember? Let's get you onto the couch so that I can examine you more thoroughly.'

After he had done so, he told her with a grin, 'No damage done as far as I can see, apart from that cut. You aren't the first pregnant mum to faint, and you won't be the last, but I suggest from now on you stop rushing around at quite your usual speed and certainly stop the mountaineering!'

'You think that's what it was? I've never fainted in my life.'

'It looks like you have now. I think we'll put one or two sutures in that wound for your beauty's sake. OK?'

Jan nodded. 'Don't bother with a local. I can bear the pain!'

'Depends who's going to do it.' Marc smiled. 'Becky?'

She pretended to check her watch and joshed for Jan's benefit, 'She's all yours, Marc. It's nearly time I was off duty. But I'll stay with you as your friend, Jan, and hold your hand.'

Marc lifted an eyebrow in resignation and Jan laughed.

'You've just got time before you start your evening surgery.'

Becky got everything ready and Marc inserted two sutures neatly and quickly. As he stripped off his gloves, he
told her, 'I think you ought to take a few more days off,
and I don't think you should drive this evening. I know
babies are well cushioned, but you don't want to give this
little mite too many shocks.'

Jan frowned. 'I can't leave my car in the car park.'

Marc looked thoughtfully at Becky. 'Would you mind
driving her home in her own car and seeing she's OK?'

She saw immediately what would happen. 'I don't mind,
Marc, but—'

'I know what you're going to say. The moment my surgery finishes I'll pick you up and bring you back to collect
your own vehicle. That's unless you have to be home earlier?'

She shook her head. 'That's fine.' Aware that under the
circumstances she could do nothing but shelve her personal
objections, she added to herself, I suppose.

She guessed Marc intended to continue their rudely interrupted chat when he picked her up and now she'd had
time to think rationally about the events of the day, she
knew she was probably as much to blame as he was. She
wondered if she should invite him to take up his rain-check
cup of coffee?

As she unlocked Jan's car and helped her friend into the
passenger seat, she mulled quickly over the events of the
day and decided coffee would not be a good idea. The
sooner she thought of Marc as nothing more than the practice principal the better. But even as the words formed in
her mind she knew it was too late for that.

'Comfortable?' she asked Jan as she started the engine.

'Totally pampered and I'm lapping it up. It's a novelty

at the moment, but I don't think I'll cope with nine months of it.'

Becky laughed. 'Don't worry about that. I can promise you it won't last!'

Jan was happily settled in an armchair when her husband arrived home from work. He was horrified when he first heard what had happened, but calmed down as Becky reassured him there was no problem with the baby.

He told Jan not to move and said he would see to everything. 'Will you stay for supper, Becky?'

'No, thanks. Dr Johnson will pick me up the moment his surgery finishes. You go ahead, though, and forget I'm here.'

As they chatted, Mike hovered anxiously around Jan, and their obvious care for one another affected Becky in the same way that the antenatal clinic had on Tuesday. She felt a huge emptiness snake through her body, a reaction that she didn't recall ever experiencing before she'd started at Sandley.

She was relieved when Marc rang the front doorbell and she could escape the couple's loving togetherness.

Marc quickly checked Jan was all right, then led Becky out to his car. 'No argument, now. I made you miss lunch and have delayed your preparations for supper so, unless you have a pressing prior arrangement, I'm treating you to a slap-up meal this evening.'

Still debating in her mind about the coffee invitation, Becky was taken aback and stuttered, 'Y-you d-don't have to do that.'

Before he started the car, he turned to look at her, an odd reflective expression in his dark eyes. 'But I want to. Don't you realise that?'

Again that empty feeling clenched at her stomach as the heat of his gaze spread through her with a remembered warmth. Did he mean it, or was he just mouthing empty words to excuse his loss of control at Paddocks?

'Something to eat would be lovely,' she answered, and determined to keep her response light-hearted and impersonal, added, 'My stomach feels as if my throat is cut.'

Even as she uttered the platitude, she recognised with relief the truth of it. That was the explanation for the sensations that had assailed her earlier.

She saw disappointment flash across his face at her evasion of his question, but he set the car in motion and told her, 'I thought we might go to the Haunted Barn.'

Becky was horrified. She didn't know many places in the area yet, but the reputation of the Barn was renowned. 'I can't go dressed like this.' She looked down at the jeans and sweater she had changed into before leaving the health centre.

'It's Monday. The Barn has a jeans night. Didn't you know that?'

'No. I've never been there. Even so, I expect people look smart.'

Again he turned the heated gaze of his dark eyes on her and they spoke much louder than his words. 'You look fine to me.'

She could argue no more because he pulled up into the Barn car park at that moment.

He replaced his own jacket with a sweater that was on the back seat and smiled. 'Will I do?'

She nodded and followed him into the nearly empty restaurant. They were shown to a secluded table for two, overlooking the extensive garden.

Becky relaxed, intending to enjoy her meal.

Marc must have sensed her tension evaporating because he smiled warmly. 'That's better.'

The food was as superb as Becky had expected from the

Barn's reputation—three courses, cheese and then coffee. Marc leaned across the table and took her hands in his. 'How's your stomach now? Still full of butterflies?'

Now why had he said that? Did he know the effect he had on her?

'I think I might just about last out until morning!'

He accepted her jokey response with a wry smile. 'Thank goodness for that. I'd hate to see that neat waistline of yours disappear.'

'I don't think there's much danger of that,' she retorted. 'I'm well aware it would earn your disapproval.'

He frowned. 'How come?'

She shrugged. 'You made it quite clear at my interview that you expect healthy eating patterns and fitness from your patients. And employees.'

He released her hands and his eyes widened with surprise. 'I did?'

'You certainly did.'

He shook his head in disbelief. 'I don't remember doing that.'

'You reinforced it when you introduced me to Sally. You were very derogatory about her weight.'

'I disapprove of her being over-fed and under-exercised when she doesn't have a say in the matter, but I certainly didn't intend to give you that impression about my patients—or staff for that matter.'

He looked hurt at the suggestion and she wondered if she had overreacted to his comments at the interview and, if so, why. Had it been because she'd already been aware of an undercurrent of attraction between them and, being a generous size twelve, had taken what he'd said personally?

If so, it was rather churlish of her to accuse him unjustly after the meal they had just enjoyed. 'Perhaps I was tense and unusually sensitive that day.'

'So I'm not the only one who jumps to conclusions,' he teased, as he again covered her hands with his own and looked deep into her eyes for confirmation.

'It seems not,' she agreed ruefully, struggling to meet his gaze without flinching.

They only pulled apart when the waiter offered them a refill of coffee. When she refused, Marc asked for the bill.

Before he set the car in motion, he turned towards her. 'While we can't be overheard or interrupted, I do want to explain about Carol and Simon. Would you mind?'

Becky shook her head.

'When I first saw Carol after her discharge from hospital, she was hysterically adamant that I tell no one what she had done. She was so ashamed after all our help and hated the thought that we'd think she'd let Simon down.'

Becky frowned, 'Difficult.'

'I know. Rose knew already. She took the message from the hospital. Anyway, I explained to Carol that there would be discharge letters, but that everyone employed by the practice was a professional whose confidentiality could be guaranteed.

'When she knew that, she wanted me to promise that only I would visit her. She said she couldn't face anyone else. She was so unstable that I didn't promise, but agreed to try—at least in the immediate future. That was when I gave her my bleeper number rather than have her call the centre when I wasn't there.'

'Was that wise?'

'I really felt I was getting somewhere, especially when she agreed to Simon being present when we discussed why she'd taken such drastic action.

'Apparently they did go to one meeting of the MS society and Simon got talking to someone in remission like himself. When he discovered all this chap was doing, especially some of the holidays he had taken, Simon decided he was missing a golden opportunity. So he gave Carol an ultimatum. Either she agreed to him doing the same, or he'd take off and travel the world on his own.

'He says he didn't threaten to leave her. He actually wanted her to be with him, whatever he did. But she was so uptight that she misunderstood.'

'That was when she rang me?'

'Probably. I'm afraid in the beginning she blamed you for everything, Becky. Totally irrational, but you had suggested the MS society chairman should visit them, and she had to find someone to blame.

'That was the reason I didn't want you to come with me when Carol bleeped me at the drug do.'

'And why you refused to tell me anything the next day?'

He gave her an embarrassed grin. 'Ah, well, I didn't think you were to be trusted then, did I?'

Becky felt a wave of dejection sweep over her. It seemed she hadn't been such a success at Sandley after all. 'Perhaps it would be better for all concerned if I look for another post.'

He must have heard the catch in her voice and took both her hands in his. 'Becky, I'm trying to explain only because I believe you deserve the truth. I certainly don't want you to leave, and now she's got the anger out of her system neither does Carol. I told you they are getting on so much better since everything is out in the open between them, and they have even booked a holiday together.'

'I'm pleased about that.'

'You'll like this, too. She said this afternoon that she had you to thank for it.'

Becky shook her head and sighed. She was exhausted after a day of her emotions swinging from one end of the scale to the other and she was finding it difficult to take in all he was telling her.

He must have sensed her weariness. 'You're tired. I'll take you back to your car, Becky. You've had one hell of a day.'

She wanted to ask whose fault that was, but she didn't have the energy. She just wanted to get home so that she could think objectively about her position at Sandley, and about Marc.

He drove her to the health centre to retrieve her car, and as he helped her into it he bent his head and kissed her— a very different kiss to the one he'd pressed upon her that afternoon. 'Thank you for listening and, I hope, understanding, and thank you for a very pleasant evening,' he whispered into her hair. 'I hope you enjoyed it, despite my disapproval of your healthy appetite!'

'It was wonderful, thanks.' She climbed behind her steering wheel and murmured, 'I'll see you tomorrow.'

At Marc's insistence, Jan took the remainder of the week off, which meant Becky was occupied every moment of her working day, and she was glad of it because she no longer knew how to relate to Marc.

Despite finding it difficult to accept his reasons for not trusting her, she was no longer prepared to allow his hang-ups to drive her away from Sandley. She enjoyed her work there and even Rose seemed more amenable.

She updated the Tuesday meeting about her diabetic clinic. 'So many patients and relatives want to come along tomorrow that I'm beginning to think I've bitten off more than I can chew.'

'Don't worry about it,' Patsy told her. 'I'll be in to help and also keep an eye on Irene and the baby clinic.'

Marc's dark eyes watched her with a brooding thoughtfulness, but he said nothing, and before the meeting ended he had to rush off in answer to an emergency call.

Work seemed destined to keep them apart, and Becky suspected it was what Marc wanted. If he regretted the events of Monday, he no doubt preferred it that way.

She was surprised, therefore, when he searched her out late on Wednesday evening.

'Hi. How did the clinic go?'

'Fine.'

'You're coping with Jan away?'

She nodded. Didn't he even think her capable of doing that?

He was clearly finding her lack of response difficult. 'I, er, wondered if you would be free on Friday evening?'

She was pleased to have the perfect excuse. 'I'm afraid not. I'm visiting friends in London this weekend.'

'Pity. I've just been given some tickets for an open air production of *A Midsummer Night's Dream*.'

Much as she'd have loved to have seen it, she noted with wry amusement he was still hedging his invitations with caution.

Jan was back again the following Monday.

'You sure you're OK now?'

Jan laughed. 'You trying to take my place? Or will my being back spoil your tête à têtes with Marc?'

Becky felt herself colouring. 'Certainly not.'

'Why so defensive? You're neither of you spoken for.' She bustled off to call in the first appointment.

Although they were coping with a heavier than usual crop of Monday morning problems, Becky found enough time to tell Jan of the decision she had come to over the weekend.

'I've decided I'm not going to waste my money on rent

any longer than I have to. At lunchtime I'll slip out to the house agents and see if they've anything in my price range on offer.'

Jan nodded. 'I'm so pleased you're going to put down roots in the area. Since your arrival on the scene, Marc is slowly emerging from his self-imposed unsociability. You work so well together.'

Becky shrugged. 'Maybe, but it'll be nothing more than that until he comes to terms with the memory of his dead fiancée.'

'I don't think he's helped by his mother's reliance on him, and now her dog has died it's going to be even worse.'

Becky was appalled. 'Sally's dead? I'd no idea. When?'

CHAPTER EIGHT

'WHEN did it happen?' Becky asked again.

'This morning. Marc was just finishing his surgery when his mother rang in to say the dog had collapsed, so he rushed off to take it to the vet. Apparently it died before he got there. He rang through to see if Pete could cope with his last few patients as he didn't want to leave his mother.'

'Poor Marc.'

Jan's news removed an edge of excitement from her house-hunting trip, and she became rapidly disheartened by the price of every property she was interested in being way beyond her reach.

She was about to leave when the bored girl at the desk called her back. 'I shouldn't tell you this, but I did notice one in the paper that might suit you.' She searched around and found the previous Friday's *Gazette*.

When Becky saw the price she guessed it would soon be snapped up. 'Thanks. I'll ring them immediately.'

The girl looked surreptitiously round the office and, finding they were still alone, said, 'I'll do it for you.'

'Could I see it tonight?' Becky whispered as the number was ringing.

'Sevenish. OK?' the desk clerk queried. 'It's Mr and Mrs Snell.'

As Becky poured out her fervent thanks, the girl handed Becky the paper. 'Don't tell a soul, will you?'

On her return to the health centre, she tried to find Marc to tell him how sorry she was, but Tanya told her he wasn't coming in for the rest of the day, leaving Becky uncertain as to whether to ring him or not. She decided to wait until she saw him the next day as she was sure Rose would have been in contact.

She parked her car a little way from the house for sale just before seven that evening. She wanted to get a feel of the area and see what the building looked like outside.

She was pleasantly surprised. It was small but had a reasonable-sized garden, even though it did need some attention, she thought as she walked up to the front door and rang the bell, which was greeted by a frantic barking.

'You the one come to look at the house?'

The speaker was scruffily dressed in dirty jeans and a open-neck shirt that looked as if it could do with being shown an iron.

At Becky's nod he added, 'You'd better come in, then.'

Overcoming her distaste for the man's appearance, Becky followed him on a tour of the house, knowing at once that after an extensive spruce-up it would be perfect for her requirements.

The stairs from the tiny hall led to only two bedrooms, but she didn't need more. Granted, it did need a good clean and redecoration but she didn't mind that. Returning to the kitchen where the man and his wife were waiting, Becky gave them the answer they wanted to hear.

'It's just what I've been looking for.' She made them an offer but they said the price was so low already they were not prepared to bargain. 'We are only selling it *that* cheap because we're emigrating. We need a quick sale.'

'I think I can probably raise the full amount, but I can't do anything about it until tomorrow. I'll contact you in the evening about the deposit after I've seen about the mortgage and found a solicitor,' Becky informed them.

Shut in the front room, the dog was barking itself into a frenzy.

'You don't know anyone who wants a dog, do you? We can't take her with us and can't seem to find anyone who wants a one-year-old Labrador. She'll have to be put down otherwise.'

Becky thought about Marc's mother and said, 'I might do. I'll make some enquiries and let you know about that tomorrow evening as well.'

She told Jan about the house as soon as she saw her the next day, but Marc was busy all morning so she didn't have an opportunity to ask him about the dog.

When they met up for the practice meeting, after saying how sorry she was about Sally, she asked to be excused.

He frowned. 'We do all try to get to this weekly meeting.'

She sighed. 'I'm sorry. It's just that I've seen a house at a price I can afford, and I want to see about a mortgage before someone else snaps it up. I made the appointment early so I'll be back for the antenatals.'

'In that case, we'll let you off. Where is this house?'

Unsure of either his or his mother's reaction to a replacement dog, Becky didn't want to ask him about it in front of the others. 'I'm late already. I'll tell you all about it later.'

There were already several mums-to-be waiting when Marc appeared to start the afternoon clinic, so he didn't have a chance to ask Becky about her house-hunting until the last of them had been seen. But he didn't forget.

'Now, tell me about this house you want to buy.'

She described its situation, but if his frown was anything to go by she hadn't made it very clear. Aware that if he agreed to look at the dog he would see it for himself, she murmured, 'I have something to ask you, Marc.'

His frown was replaced by a disbelieving smile. 'You're asking for my help?'

'No…it's just…' Becky felt her colour rising as she tried to explain. 'This house I saw. The owners are emigrating and have a one-year-old Labrador they can't take with them. I wondered how your mother might feel about it?'

He sat down thoughtfully on the edge of the desk.

'I don't know, Becky. I think it might be a bit too early—'

'But if the dog would be put down otherwise?' she interrupted eagerly. 'I thought perhaps you might like to see the Labrador for yourself this evening.'

'What colour is it?'

Realising suddenly how little she had found out about the animal, she replied, 'I don't really know. It barked so much they kept moving it from room to room as I looked round, and I only heard it.'

'Hmm, doesn't sound as if it's very well trained. What was the house like?'

'It needs redecoration but that's no problem.'

'Did anyone go with you to see the house?'

'No. Why should they?'

'I hope you know what you're doing then. Have you bought a house before?'

'No, but there has to be a first time for everything and this is mine. Now, are you interested in that dog or not?' Annoyed by his attitude, Becky didn't want to discuss the house and she wished now that she had never mentioned the wretched animal.

'Yes, I'd like to see it. And the house. I'll pick you up between six and half past. If that's not too early.'

Marc was very quiet as they toured the house that evening to the incessant accompaniment of barking. When they returned downstairs he asked about the dog. When it was brought into the kitchen Becky found it difficult to believe that the thin, miserable-looking animal was indeed a golden Labrador. She looked at Marc for his reaction and was surprised to see him bend to examine the shivering animal closely from head to toe.

'I'd like to think about her. Can I let you know later in the week, Mr…er…?'

'Snell. Yes, that'll be all right. We won't be leaving till at least the end of the month.'

Marc nodded. 'I meant to ask about the cracks in the walls. Do you know the cause of them?'

'Drying-out cracks, when the house was new-like. Most people papers over the cracks when they are trying to sell, but I thinks it's fairer to let you see 'em. Are you buying the house with the young lady?'

'No, I'm buying it alone,' Becky hastened to assure him. 'He came to see the dog.'

'What about the deposit, then? Did you sort out the mortgage today?'

'More or less. I—'

'I think it best if she leaves the deposit until she's got her mortgage confirmed.'

'I—' began Becky indignantly, but Marc let her get no further. Opening the front door, he grabbed her elbow and propelled her out at speed before she even had a chance to continue the sentence.

'Just what do you think you are playing at, Marc Johnson?' Becky could hardly wait until the door closed to round on him. 'My buying the house is nothing to do with you. I just brought you to see the Labrador. What makes you think you have any right to tell me what I shall or shan't do? Why don't you keep your nose out of my business dealings? Suppose they promise the house to someone else? Someone who pays the deposit immediately?'

Gripping her arm firmly, he frogmarched her to the car and, opening the passenger door, almost pushed her inside. Remaining silent, he strode round to the other side and, ignoring Becky's furious protests, climbed into the driving seat and started the engine. He drove furiously to the car park at the reservoir.

Pulling on the handbrake, he turned to face her and said, 'Now, Becky, my love, you are not putting a deposit on that house, not today, not tomorrow and, if my suspicions are confirmed, not ever. Right?'

'No, it certainly is not all right, and I'm not your love nor are ever likely to be. I just don't believe this.' Unusually, Becky was making no attempt to curb the temper that accompanied her red hair, and she felt the colour flooding into her cheeks.

'You sit there and calmly tell me I'm not going to put a deposit on the only house I've found at a price I can afford.'

When he didn't speak immediately, she continued, 'Just what do you consider gives you the right to tell me what I shall or shan't do? I'm damned if I'm going to let you order me about in this way. You wouldn't have known anything about it if I hadn't told you about that blasted dog. What house I buy is none of your business. And—' Becky choked on her words as her fury began to evaporate, and disappointment brought tears to her eyes.

Marc slid an arm around her shoulder and said quietly, 'I'm sorry I had to rush you out that way, but it was the only thing I could think of to prevent you doing something you might regret later. If you'll just let me explain…'

'Explain away. I'm waiting.' Angrily, Becky brushed away an escaping tear.

Marc sighed deeply. 'Were you going to have a surveyor look at the house, Becky?'

Turning to glare once again at Marc, Becky was surprised to see not reciprocal anger but only concern in his brown eyes.

'That doesn't sound like an explanation to me, more like a question. And, moreover, a question I don't see why I should answer. But, as it happens, the answer is yes. I couldn't get a mortgage otherwise.' Becky intended the scathing tone of her voice to convey her total distrust of both his actions and his motives.

'That wasn't what I meant. What about a private survey? The building society don't tell you what they've found, only what price they think the house is worth.'

'Don't be ridiculous, Marc. I can't afford a private survey on top of everything else. I just don't know what you are trying to say.'

'Becky, I don't like your Mr Snell—'

'So what? He doesn't come with the house!'

'Just let me finish. Unless I'm very much mistaken, that house you are about to spend your hard-earned money on is rapidly subsiding into old mine workings.' He paused to let his information seep into Becky's consciousness. 'Also, that Labrador bitch has been very badly treated. She's so terrified I doubt if she will ever recover from the treatment she's had in that house. All in all, I think sooner or later you would have found that your Mr Snell is not to be trusted.'

'I can't see what his character has to do with it, and I don't understand what you mean about the house. I suppose it's those cracks you are referring to. But all houses have cracks when the plaster dries out. Even I know that.' Still annoyed, Becky was determined not to believe that Marc knew what he was talking about.

'I'm sorry, Becky, but I have the advantage of local knowledge. I recall a news item in the local papers about the problem and I'm pretty sure that house is one of them—'

'But you can't say for certain, can you?' In her desperation Becky was grasping at straws. When Marc didn't answer immediately she repeated insistently, 'Well, can you?'

Sighing deeply, Marc shook his head. 'All right, I know I might be wrong but I'd rather look into it before you pay a deposit than afterwards. I don't think you'd be likely to get any money back from the Snells.'

'But there's nothing else on the market I can remotely afford, Marc, I can't not put a deposit on it, knowing that someone else is likely to snap it up. What if it turns out you're wrong? It's just what I want and handy for the health centre…' This time Becky couldn't prevent her tears spilling over. Ignoring the neatly folded handkerchief Marc proffered, Becky rummaged in her handbag for a tissue.

Marc shrugged off the rebuff, saying, 'Get a survey done then, but, better still, let me make some enquiries tomorrow morning. That'll cost you nothing. If I'm wrong I'll give him the deposit personally, but I don't think I'm going to be.'

Unwilling to admit the faint possibility that Marc could be right, Becky sat in a morose silence, trying to convince herself it was sensible not to risk losing the deposit. It was money she could ill afford to lose and deep down she knew it would be foolhardy to do anything more about the house until Marc had made his enquiries. Nevertheless, her pride would not allow her to admit it so, having made up her mind that they could not sit by the water without speaking all evening, she broke the silence by asking about the dog.

'What are you going to do about the Labrador?'

'I'll have a chat with the vet about her. If necessary I'll

take him to see her. For two pins I'd call in the RSPCA immediately, but I don't want to antagonise Snell. There didn't appear to be any recent injuries on her, and I don't want him to inflict some in temper because of my actions. Come on, it's nearly eight, and I'm starving. Let's go and have something to eat. I thought we'd try the Plough again.'

Becky, who had been watching the quiet anger flicker in his eyes as he spoke, recognised that he was a man of unwavering convictions. He was unable to tolerate anyone ill-treating animals, any more than he could condone her stupidity in trying to buy a house without asking for help. His concern for both her finances and the dog revealed a caring man that made him increasingly hard to resist. In fact, he was good husband material going to waste.

'What about your mother, Marc? Won't she be expecting you this evening?'

He glanced at her with a puzzled frown. 'Why should she?'

'She must be lonely without Sally. I thought—I thought you would be spending some time with her until she gets used to the idea.'

The moment she said the words, she knew it had been a mistake.

'I'm beginning to think you jump to more wrong conclusions about me, than I do about you. I suppose I could easily have moved back into the family home when I lost Julie, but I do have a life of my own and so does my mother.'

'But…' Not wanting to make matters worse, she bit back the words she'd been about to say.

'But what? Come on, we might as well have everything out in the open.'

'It was just when you mentioned the Plough. I remembered the first time we went there you said you sometimes took your mother there for Sunday lunch because you don't find enough time to spend with her. I—I suppose I presumed she was lonely in that big house.'

'I'm sure she'd much prefer to have my father still with her, but she's so busy working and socialising with the members of various local organisations that it's impossible for us to find a mutually free weekday to meet up. That's why I take her out for Sunday lunch. It's the only chance I get to see her.'

Realising her mistake, Becky saw that her belief that he'd surface quicker from his grief without his mother to remind him of the accident was way off the mark.

'Is the Plough all right then?'

'It's fine by me.' As things stood, Becky would have agreed, whatever his suggestion.

The smell of home cooking as they entered the bar was like a soothing balm to Becky's turmoil. The food was as good as on their previous visit, and they chatted about work and Paddocks, but kept off the subject of the house for sale. Marc proved himself once again a charming companion and Becky's heart warmed to him all over again.

When they reached her flat afterwards, he took her hand to help her from the car.

'Thanks for the evening, Marc. You will let me know immediately if you discover there is nothing wrong with the house, then…?'

He was clearly annoyed at her feeling the need to confirm he would do as she wanted. 'I promised I'd put the deposit on it personally if I do, and I don't break my promises. I'll be in touch.'

He stood for a moment as if undecided, then, pulling her roughly to him, he lowered his lips to hers and kissed her. A kiss that was hard, long and probing. And as she parted her lips to allow his tongue to tangle with hers, she felt her body respond.

He released her almost at the same moment that Becky had abandoned all hope of breathing again. He stood back, still holding her lightly, and scrutinised her face. 'Oh, Becky. What am I going to do?'

Giddy and bemused, Becky was about to offer that neglected rain check when he abruptly released the hand he was holding and said, 'Goodnight, Becky. I'll see you in the morning.' He strode to his car and drove off without looking back.

As she watched his car lights disappear, she scrutinised the events of the evening from every direction, but could not come up with any reason for his abrupt departure.

Unless...unless he was regretting that kiss. Which was more than likely when, apart from this evening, every invitation had had an ulterior motive—in fact, their outing this evening had only been a follow-up to them viewing the house together.

Yet, if Jan was to be believed, she wasn't the only one to have noticed the attraction between them. So if, as he'd said, there was no pressure from his mother, his reluctance to become involved again must solely be because he wasn't prepared to risk being hurt again.

Did he think that was likely to happen? Did he still not trust her sufficiently?

She made her way indoors and to bed no nearer an answer, and she spent a disturbed night, dreaming first that Paddocks disappeared into a coal mine, then that Mr Snell was attacking Marc and the dog with a roll of house plans. Awakening with a start and seeing it was only six-thirty, she decided on a leisurely bath, before setting out for work.

Jan was back in form and saw many of the patients the

next morning, so Becky wasn't able to immerse herself in her work sufficiently to forget her problems.

When she had finally completed her preparations for the afternoon diabetic clinic, Tanya handed her a note from Marc. It wasn't good news. The house *was* one of those affected by subsidence. The stilted note concluded that he would give her the details later.

She made her way into the coffee-room trying to stem the flow of tears her disappointment threatened—partly over the house, but partly at Marc's impersonal way of telling her.

Jan looked up. 'Everything OK?'

She shook her head and scrumpled the note in her hand. 'That house I'd set my heart on. It's subsiding. Into mine workings. Marc says he'll be in touch later with the details.'

Jan nodded. 'He probably couldn't wait to tell you himself because he was taking Rose out to lunch. He asked me to tell you that he wouldn't be sitting in on the diabetic session this afternoon.'

Becky couldn't believe what Jan was telling her. Mark had made such a point of informing her that Rose was chasing him and not the other way around. She had to swallow hard to keep the still threatening tears at bay as she recognised her mistake of the night before. It wasn't that Marc couldn't trust her. It was Becky who shouldn't trust Marc.

Her diabetic clinic was busy and ran on till nearly five. She hadn't expected it to grow so rapidly, but the number of patients attending was vindication of her request to set it up.

'It's such a drag to the hospital,' one of the first female patients that afternoon told her. 'Two buses and then a long wait unless you're lucky. When I saw the notice about you, I cancelled my hospital appointment immediately.'

That afternoon, Becky doled out her health education and dietary advice with very little enthusiasm. She didn't see Marc until he arrived back at the health centre for his evening surgery.

'I'm sorry about the house, Becky,' he told her hurriedly, 'but everyone I've spoken to advises against you even considering it. Snell is trying to pull a fast one, hoping to unload the house on some unsuspecting newcomer to the area. That's why he's offering it cheap. Probably the building society would have turned it down anyway but, just in case, it's best for you to know.' He handed her a file of photocopies.

'Thank you. It's very kind of you to go to all this trouble,' she told him stonily.

He looked at her closely and took her arm. 'Don't be downhearted. There'll be other houses, I'm sure. And probably in much better areas.'

'I didn't see a lot wrong with where this one is sited.'

Unaware that her pique had been caused by anything more than disappointment over the house, Marc's smile was open and friendly. 'That doesn't surprise me. You haven't lived here long enough to know as yet.'

Becky was so disappointed and so jealous that she ignored the even tenor of his voice and muttered, 'Don't be so patronising, Marc.'

He took a surprised step back. 'I certainly didn't mean to be. Look, I'm sorry I can't talk now. I've patients waiting. Perhaps—'

'No problem,' she told him. 'I have to rush as well. I have to be in Begstone before seven.'

She flounced away leaving Marc immobile with surprise. What on earth had triggered that outburst? She'd seemed eventually to accept that his efforts on her behalf were in her best interest so he'd gone to great lengths to make absolutely sure he wasn't mistaken about the house.

And after the kiss they'd shared the previous night, he'd known there was no way he wanted to proceed with caution a moment longer. Before he made a move, however, he wanted to make it perfectly clear to Rose exactly how he felt—or rather didn't feel—about her, or ever had.

He had invited Rose to lunch and over their food had discovered she was well on the way to accepting that they were nothing more than good friends. She had even wished him luck. When he mentioned his meetings with Tony, she had confessed to regretting their separation and had asked Marc for his help in getting them together one evening. That was something he was very happy to do.

He'd come back confident that Rose would no longer make life difficult for Becky, and itching to invite her out on a proper date for the first time, only to have her accuse him of being patronising!

And to tell him that she had a date of some sort in Begstone that evening. He shook his head despairingly. Surely he hadn't been wrong all along about her feeling as he did? He'd sensed the magnetism between them the moment she'd walked into the interview room, and as he'd got to know her better his feelings had grown into a love he now wanted to share. But it seemed he might have left it too late. As well as making too many mistakes on the way. Surely after five years he was entitled to a little happiness?

Angrily he snatched up his notes from Reception, and made his way into his consulting room, slamming the door behind him.

Becky drove home slowly, her eyes wet with unshed tears. Jan had saved her from making a complete fool of herself.

She'd been near to it the previous evening, and if Jan hadn't told her about his lunchtime date with Rose she'd probably have gone on to do so properly that evening. She was pretty sure he'd been about to ask her out to chat about the house once he'd finished his surgery.

Thank goodness for the library! He need never know that was her only pressing date that evening, or any other for that matter. Though she intended to change that at once. She'd been so taken with Marc that she hadn't given a thought to creating a social life for herself in Sandley or Begstone. Work and Marc had been more than enough for her. But that was about to change. The library would have lists of local organisations, which would enable her to set about making a life for herself unconnected with the health centre.

When she reached her flat, complete with addresses and telephone numbers, she rang her mother and arranged to go home for the weekend.

'About time, too,' Mrs Groom said reproachfully. 'I'm looking forward to hearing all about Paddocks and how Doris Bennett and Martha Lewin are getting on.'

Becky replaced the receiver and sighed. She hoped she'd survive the weekend of questions she knew she was going to be subjected to.

She was making herself an omelette when the telephone rang. Rather than ruin her meal, she let the answerphone take the call and was glad she had done so when she heard it was Marc. He was the last person she wanted to hear from or meet up with that evening. The next morning at work would be soon enough.

Jan had taken Thursday morning off and was working the evening shift as Irene had a parents' evening at school. It meant Becky was kept busy all day as she had her well-person clinic list in the afternoon.

The only patient she needed to consult a doctor about was on Pete's list, so the first time she encountered Marc was at lunchtime when she was clearing the treatment room at the end of the morning list.

'Hi,' he greeted her as she changed the sheet on the treatment couch. 'I'm sure you'll be pleased to know that the plans are completed and going to the planning office this afternoon. Would you like to have a quick look at them first?'

'I'm afraid I don't have the time. My well-person clinic begins in ten minutes.' She moved from the couch to her desk without meeting his eyes.

'That's a pity. I thought you might have some last-minute comments.'

She shrugged. 'It's no big deal. It was just a house I once knew.'

Believing this must be her repayment for his interference in her house purchase, he said, 'I'm really sorry to have spoilt your first excursion into home ownership, Becky. I only had your financial well-being at heart.'

She nodded, but didn't answer.

'Perhaps it would have been better if I'd left you to fight your own battles.'

Again the silent nod.

'I've no surgery this evening, so could we meet and chat about it?'

Becky shook her head, relieved not to have to lie this time. 'Sorry, I've arranged to play badminton.' She'd rung the secretary of a club from her library list earlier that morning and they'd jumped at her request to join, especially when they heard she had once played for her school team.

'Tomorrow evening, then?'

'As soon as I finish here I'm going home to Shropshire for the weekend.'

'So when will you be free to discuss it?' he asked suspiciously.

'Monday or Tuesday next week—that's if I haven't a badminton match. I won't know until this evening.'

He strode off, fuming at her obvious intention to keep him at arm's length.

Becky enjoyed her first visit to the badminton club. Everyone was friendly, and when they learned she was new to the district she was showered with invitations to other events.

It was just the confidence-booster she needed before she drove home to endure her mother's cross-examination about Paddocks, her flat, her work and, most of all, about the senior partner who rang her at home. The questions about Marc were the hardest to deal with because she found it difficult to hide her hurt feelings from her mother, but as she drove back to Begstone on Sunday evening she congratulated herself on having succeeded.

'Now all you have to do is convince *yourself* you don't care,' she muttered to herself, well aware that she was asking the near impossible.

Laura came to see her at the end of a busy Monday morning session in the treatment room. She was excited as she confided, 'I've just been to see Marc and I thought you'd like to know. I'm going for another baby. The IVF team say it should be much less hassle than last time as we have an embryo stored.'

'That's great, Laura. I *do* hope it's a success.'

'I'm so excited. I want to tell everyone.' She gave Becky a bear hug. 'Now, tell me, how are things progressing between you and Marc?'

'In the way you mean, Laura, they aren't. We work well together, but that's all.'

Laura stared at her, wide-eyed. 'You can't mean that!'

'I'm afraid so.'

'Andrew hasn't given me that impression at all. We'll have to see what we can do.'

Becky shrugged and watched her leave with a heavy heart. Laura's concern for Marc and her excitement about her plans for another baby had reduced Becky to a quivering mass of unhappiness. She could perhaps fool everyone else, but not herself.

She managed to keep well out of Marc's way until the practice meeting on Tuesday, and even then she found herself a seat between Patsy and Steve and managed to avoid meeting Marc's eyes once.

Later that afternoon Becky answered the surgery phone as she was making coffee for herself and Emma at the end of the antenatal clinic.

'Emergency,' she heard Rose bellow in her ear. 'And there are no doctors in. He's collapsed, hitting his head as he fell. He's unconscious.' Her voice was rising to a hysterical level.

CHAPTER NINE

BECKY was already collecting her resuscitation equipment.

'What happened?'

'Hit his head I think,' one of the bystanders replied. 'Just fainted probably.'

'Has anybody called an ambulance?' she asked as calmly as she could.

'It's on its way.'

She noticed Marc arriving as she was checking the casualty's breathing and heart rate. He crouched down beside her. 'Anything I can do to help?'

Before Becky could reply, the patient began to cough and splutter. Ceasing her efforts, she quickly checked for other injuries, then, making sure the casualty was breathing satisfactorily, prepared to turn him with Marc's help into the recovery position.

'You're all right, Simon. Just take it easy.'

'Simon?' Becky mouthed. 'You know him?'

'Simon Dent,' he told her as an ambulance arrived. 'I'll go with him in the ambulance, Becky. Would you mind following and bringing me back to the car park?'

She could do nothing but agree.

When he finally appeared from the hospital, he thanked her for waiting. 'X-ray has revealed no fractures, but because of his history they've admitted him overnight for observation. He's fine now. I'm more than glad you were there when it happened, Becky.'

She refused to allow herself to succumb to his blandishments. 'Would you like me to go and tell Carol what's happened?'

'I think it's probably best if I explain personally how he was when I left him, and why it's important they keep him in for observation.' He gave her a quizzical look. 'Perhaps it would be a good idea if we both go.'

For Carol's sake she didn't argue.

As they had both expected, Carol was at first distraught, blaming herself. Becky made her a cup of tea, while Marc struggled to persuade her that it was nothing more than an unfortunate accident. 'Simon said he'd gone to the surgery to save you a trip to pick up his usual prescription. His very words were, ''Pride goes before a fall because I was trying to prove I could manage without my glasses and I missed the step.'''

His words brought a fresh bout of weeping from Carol, 'The poor darling. He's so vain about wearing them.'

When she'd finished drinking the cup of tea Becky had made, she'd calmed down and wanted to go and visit him.

'Are you sure you're OK driving?'

Carol laughed. 'I'm not the one trying to manage without glasses.'

When Marc and Becky had taken their leave he smiled and tentatively suggested they stop for a meal.

Becky tried to refuse what she saw as another meal of convenience.

'It's not your badminton night, is it?'

'No, but I seem to be making a habit of accepting your hospitality.' Just like Rose, she added silently.

'I told you last week I want to do it. I hate to think of you rushing home to prepare a meal after I've made you work such long hours.'

Put that way, it was difficult to refuse. Resigned, she drove straight to the little bistro they had tried once before.

At least she had the car tonight and could drop him back at the car park and escape immediately.

After they'd ordered he brought up the subject of the house. 'I've discovered the Snells are trying to unload the house before it's too late.'

'Aren't they really emigrating, then?' Becky asked.

'Apparently not.'

'So what about the dog? Why is he trying to get rid of it?'

'I should think she has just become an expensive nuisance. However, when you agreed you wouldn't go ahead with the purchase of the house, I contacted the RSPCA about her. The vet said that was the best thing to do. I told them I'm willing to consider her as a companion for Mum if she settles down sufficiently.'

'I do hope it works out for them both.' Becky murmured, wishing that just occasionally her own plans did.

Marc must have heard the sadness in her voice. 'That house would have been a millstone round your neck.'

She smiled to hide the truth that the thought of losing him was causing her more heartache than the house. 'I know that now, and I'm grateful you stopped me when you did.'

The food arrived and their chatter became sporadic. When they'd finished the meal she said brightly, 'Another early start tomorrow. OK if I drop you back at the health centre now?'

He subjected her to one of his intense dark looks, but she jumped up and he could do nothing but follow her out to the car.

'Becky, if it's not the house that's making you so angry with me, what is it?'

Hardly able to believe he was asking, she started up the engine and forced the car into gear. 'I'm not angry.'

'So why are you taking it out on the gears?' he asked quietly as the lever grated into fourth.

'My clutch is going.'

'I'm not surprised if you knock the teeth off it at that rate.'

'Very funny,' she spat out. 'Is there anything else about me you'd like to criticise while you're about it?'

'Becky! The last thing I want to do is criticise anything about you. Surely I've made that clear by now—'

'Clear as mud,' she snapped as she swung the car into the health centre car park. He leaned across and kissed her lightly on the cheek. 'Becky…' he cried out as she pulled deliberately away from him. Unable to forget him lunching with Rose, she could take no more. 'Sorry, Marc. I'm expecting a phone call. I must dash.'

He climbed out of the car and she sped off, the tears streaming down her cheeks.

'Lost your appetite?' Jan teased on Friday lunchtime as for the second day running Becky resealed most of the sandwich she had brought.

'I'm not hungry.'

'I know Marc's fanatical about fitness, but you don't need to diet. It must be love,' said Jan.

Becky tried to hide her own disquiet. Since she had dropped him off at the health centre to pick up his car late on Tuesday evening, Marc had been conspicuously absent whenever Becky had had a free moment.

If he was regretting his declaration on Tuesday evening, he didn't have to worry. Becky had made up her mind that that was the last meal of convenience she would accept from him. Unlike Rose, she had her pride.

She was surprised, then, when early in the afternoon he

rang and asked her to come to his consulting room when she had a moment.

Friday again. What had she done this time? Surely it couldn't be anything to do with the Dents. She'd been pleased to hear that Simon had been discharged from hospital the day before, but she didn't think it was her place to initiate a visit.

She knocked on his open door and he looked up with a smile. 'Come in, Becky. I'm glad to see you.' Coming forward to meet her he grasped her hand and said jokingly, 'I haven't seen you for a couple of days. I did wonder if your loss of appetite for lunch had resulted in you fading away to nothing.' He squeezed her hand as if to prove to himself there was no danger of such a thing happening.

Unprepared again for her reaction to his touch, Becky was grateful to sit down in the chair indicated, before attempting to answer him. 'I haven't lost my appetite, but it's too hot at lunchtimes to want much.' She looked up at him suspiciously. 'Anyway, how did you know? I haven't seen you in the coffee-room all week.'

He grinned. 'The grapevine, of course. I don't think I miss anything that goes on in this place.'

She nodded ruefully. 'I'd better not help myself from the drug cupboard, then.'

'And your lunchtimes have been busy, searching fruitlessly for another house you can afford.'

She met his searching gaze and answered irritably, 'If you already know, why the inquisition?'

'Hey, Becky. Lighten up. I'm just excited by some news I have.'

She waited expectantly.

'Mr Brown has decided to move up with his niece in Scotland.'

'Is he back?' Becky's first thought was for his dressing.

'No. He's handling the sale at long distance. His niece rang me. He's registering with a doctor up in Scotland and is already having his dressings done there.'

'That's great news. It's sad to think of people being as lonely as he was.'

He shook his head slowly. 'Haven't you thought what this might mean to you?'

'His house will be for sale.' Horrified, Becky lifted a hand to her mouth. 'I didn't suggest he give Scotland a try for that reason.'

'You little goose,' Marc pushed the door closed and lifted her into his arms. 'I wasn't accusing you—far from it. I don't think I've ever known anyone whose thoughts are always for others. You never think of yourself, do you?'

He pulled her close and as his mouth covered hers she felt the excitement in his lean, hard body.

'Marc!' she protested when she could draw a breath. 'Someone might come in.'

He smiled mischievously, 'Let them. If you won't accept any of my invitations, I'll have to take my chances where and when I can.' He reluctantly released her. 'I suppose you're right. We can continue this after we've taken a look at Alan's house. He wants you to have first refusal, so I've made an appointment for ten tomorrow.'

Remembering her decision to accept no more outings of convenience, she murmured, 'I wouldn't want to spoil your day off. I can manage by myself.'

His answering sigh was so deep and melancholy that Becky took a surprised step backwards.

When he did speak, he ground out the words. 'I owe it to you, as it was my fault you didn't proceed with the Snells' house.'

She'd been right, then. Becky's disappointment at him

confirming the reason for his offer tore through her body like a knife.

'You owe me nothing.' She opened the door to leave, then turned. 'Do I have to collect the key?'

'We're meeting the house agent on the premises at ten. I'll see you there.'

Becky turned to leave and said over her shoulder, 'Don't worry if you can't make it for any reason. I'll understand.'

'Which is more than I do,' Marc muttered as he lowered his head into his hands. What did he have to do to convince her of his growing love for her?

She only agreed to share a meal with him if he had a plausible reason for inviting her—like keeping her late at work, or at the hospital.

She'd rebuffed the only invitations he'd issued when there hadn't been a good reason—pretending she was going to play badminton, when he'd never heard her mention it before.

His thoughts were disturbed by the telephone. It was the planning officer he'd been dealing with since they'd made the decision about Paddocks.

'Marc. It's not good news, I'm afraid.'

'What's the problem?'

'The planning committee has rejected your plans out of hand.'

Shaken by the totally unexpected news, he asked, 'Why? You were in favour of it.'

'I was, and so were my colleagues. But the planning committee is a totally different kettle of fish. One of the members saw the piece in the *Gazette* and had whipped most of the others into agreement with him even before I presented the plans. We didn't stand a chance.'

'But why was he so against it?'

'You tell me. He itemised a whole list of reasons why it

was a bad idea, his main objection being that he thought it should remain a home, even if it had to be divided into flats. Said it epitomised the true character of the region. I pointed out that your plans would retain the outer façade as it stands, but he insisted that once the building was sold and permission given for change of use the council would have no say in its preservation.'

'But that's not true. We would still have to apply for planning permission.'

'I pointed that out as well and there wasn't one other reason that I considered merited outright rejection. But I was wrong. There could be a hidden agenda, I suppose.'

Marc's heart sank. 'Is there anything we can do?'

'There is just a chance that the full council will overturn the decision next week, but I very much doubt it. He's got too many councillors backing him. I'll send you a copy of his reasons, but I doubt if you'll make any sense of it.'

'Thanks for all you've done. I know it's not your fault.' Marc replaced the receiver and sank back into his chair, defeated.

Just as he thought he was getting his life back together, it was falling even further apart. First Becky's disinterest and now this. What had he ever done to deserve such rotten luck?

'Problem?' Jan asked when Becky slammed the door on her return to the treatment room.

Aware that her face must have made her feelings obvious, Becky told her. 'Alan Brown's house is up for sale. Marc has persuaded the agent to give me first refusal tomorrow and has made an appointment for us both to see it at ten.'

'So what's wrong with that?'

'I'm never going to be able to make a life for myself with him around.'

Jan laughed. 'I told you so. I don't know why you're bothering to look for a house. He'd probably agree to you moving in with him tomorrow.'

'Jan!' Becky was scandalised. 'For goodness' sake, don't say such things.'

'Why not? You're both free adults, past the age of consent, and Marc surely deserves some happiness in the future. You're obviously the one to provide it, so why wait?'

'You've got it all wrong. You want everybody to have a happy ending like you. But Marc isn't the one to provide it for me.'

'Rubbish, Becky, I've seen the way he looks at you.'

'Maybe, but that's because he's lonely. Nothing more. I mean it, Jan. I thought the same as you in the beginning, until I realised he never asked me out unless he had the security of a good reason for us to get together. First it was to show me Paddocks, then because Laura and Andrew asked us. He even used you. We went out for a meal after you fell, but only because it was late when he picked me up at your house.'

'But—'

'Surely you can see, Jan,' she broke in. 'He's afraid. Afraid to commit himself in case something snatches away his happiness again. Whether it's with Rose or me, until he accepts that Julie's death was nothing more than a tragic accident he'll never make a successful relationship. And however attracted to him I am, and he may be to me, I can't afford to wait. Do you understand?'

'I suppose so.' Jan hugged her warmly. 'I just wish there was something I could do.'

'There isn't. It's up to Marc now. That's why I'd rather

go and look at this house on my own tomorrow. I just feel he's using it as one more excuse to be with me.'

'So what are you going to do?'

Becky shrugged. 'I don't want to create tension at work, so there's nothing I can do about viewing the house with him, but I don't have to accept his suggestion that we go on to lunch, or anything else.'

Jan shook her head sadly. 'It seems such a waste.'

'It would be a greater waste if I allowed him further into my life and then found I couldn't cope with his anxieties. That would just feed his insecurity.'

Jan nodded and checked her watch. 'One of us had better start seeing the patients on this afternoon's list. We've been getting busier and busier since your arrival on the scene.'

'I'll make a start,' Becky offered. 'Why don't you catch up on all the paperwork and then go home? You've had a busy week.'

Jan nodded. 'That sounds good. I wasn't looking forward to sharing my job with you, but you're the best thing that could have happened.'

Becky only had four patients that afternoon, but they all took longer than she expected so Irene was already on duty by the time she could escape for another date with the Begstone library.

She was up bright and early the next morning, and although there was an early heat haze it was obvious it was going to be another gloriously sunny day. Having taken her time over breakfast and the few chores she needed to do, Becky suddenly realised she was going to be late if she didn't hurry.

She changed quickly into what she decided was the coolest outfit in her wardrobe—a lime green sleeveless dress and sandals.

She arrived at Alan Brown's house just after ten past ten,

flustered and apologetic. She was surprised that Marc didn't comment on her lateness, but merely introduced her to the house agent.

'Now you're here,' the dapper little man told her impatiently, 'we can get started.'

Becky had seen the living area and the kitchen when she had brought Alan home, but she hadn't seen the bedrooms. Marc followed them round, but made no comment.

As they came back down the stairs she turned to him and enthused, 'It's ideal, isn't it, Marc? Just right for me.'

He nodded but didn't speak and Becky was suddenly aware that his excitement of the day before was missing, and wondered what she had missed. 'Have you seen some snags?' she asked fearfully.

He shook his head, but his voice was toneless as he said, 'It obviously needs redecorating throughout, but that should be no problem.'

Puzzled, she looked up at him and was surprised by the pain she thought she could read in his eyes. What on earth had happened? She wanted to ask him, but she knew she would have to wait. She dragged her eyes from his face to the information sheet the estate agent had handed her, and asked quietly, 'So, do you think it's a good price?'

'If it's what you want. Can you raise that sort of money?'

'I—I don't think there should be any problem.' He was clearly so dejected that she was no longer sure if it was what she wanted. She just wished to be rid of the agent so that she could find out what the matter was.

'Can I come by your office later and let you know definitely?'

The agent appeared displeased. 'I need your decision by Monday morning at the latest. You have been given the first refusal, but if you don't want it I must get the details into the paper.'

Becky felt her cheeks colour at the criticism in his voice. 'I do understand and I'll try and let you know one way or the other before the day is out, otherwise at nine on Monday morning.'

'We close at twelve today so make it Monday. Nine sharp,' he said reprovingly as he locked up and set off down the path.

'Thank you very much,' Becky called after him.

She turned to Marc and in an attempt to cheer him up said, 'He's certainly one of the old school. I don't think I'm the flavour of the month, do you?'

When Marc didn't respond, either with a smile or a word, she grasped his hand. 'Is something wrong Marc?'

All her resolutions of the day before were forgotten at the sight of his misery. Whatever it was that had happened to change his mood so dramatically overnight, she longed to wrap her arms around him and comfort him.

But here wasn't the place, and when he didn't respond, she asked quietly, 'Would you like that rain-check cup of coffee?'

He nodded. 'That would be very kind, but hadn't you better see about your mortgage?'

He might have been talking to a passer-by.

'There's plenty of time. My appointment at the bank isn't till twelve forty-five and it's not far to my flat from here. Where's your car?'

'I walked.'

'It'll have to be mine, then.' She took his arm and led him to her trusty Mini.

Once they were under way, she stole a look at his impassive face and asked again, 'Was there something you weren't happy with in the house?'

'Nothing. It's perfect for you. An opportunity not to be

missed,' he told her with the first flash of animation she had seen that morning.

'Do you think the asking price is fair, or should I haggle?'

'I don't think you can afford to haggle unless the mortgage surveyor says it's worth very much less.'

'I'm very grateful to you for arranging for me to see it.'

'I think Alan Brown would like you to have it.'

She smiled demurely as she braked the car in front of her flat. 'I'm sure he won't care who buys it as long as he gets the money.'

'I don't know about that. He's lived in it since he was born.'

He helped her from the driver's seat and, taking her keys, locked up the car. When they reached the front door, he opened it for her.

'I'm afraid it's a long climb,' she told him. 'No lift.'

'Are you suggesting I'm unfit?' He grinned, giving her a fleeting glimpse of the Marc she thought she knew.

'Would I dare?' she murmured as she led the way up to her third-floor flat.

'What a fantastic view,' he called to her as she was priming the coffee-maker.

'I'll be quite sorry to leave it.' She had moved to his side.

'I can imagine.' He turned to look at her, his eyes appearing black against the light. 'Do you think you'll be happy in Alan's little house?'

'I don't see why not.'

She watched as he compressed his lips and turned again to the view.

'You'll have nothing to compare with this. The cottage is overlooked on all sides.'

'I know. But it'll be my own. It would be silly to waste money on rent just for a view.'

'I guess so.'

'Anyway, I'll have plenty of views from the new surgery when we move to Paddocks.'

He inhaled deeply and moved across to an easy chair. 'Ah, well, that's not going to happen.'

Wondering if she'd heard aright, she swung round from the window and said, 'Did you say it wasn't going to happen?'

He nodded. 'The planning committee have thrown it out. We're going to have to restart our search.'

Recognising the reason for his long face, she struggled to find words that would express her own devastation at his news. True, she'd reacted badly when she'd first heard of his plans for the house, but now she'd become so involved with the idea that she could almost envisage what it would have looked like.

'They can't do that, Marc.'

'I'm afraid they can and they have. Their decision still has to be ratified by the full council, but they aren't likely to disagree. Especially as Pete told me this morning that a petition to keep the health centre where it is has been circulating the local shops.'

'Because of the piece in the *Gazette*?'

He nodded. 'Which I now gather was leaked by someone in the planning office who caught a glimpse of the rough drawings I took to my early discussions with the planning officer.'

'But why are all the planners so against Paddocks, Marc? It's been empty for so long. No one else wants it. I was so looking forward to it being warm and lived-in again, and now it's going to be dumped back into its dusty neglect. We can't let them get away with this.'

Her outburst warmed his shuttered face for a moment. 'And I thought you still resented my desecration of your beloved Paddocks.'

She stomped into the kitchen and poured them both a mug of coffee and placed one in front of him. She curled up on the settee with her hands clasped round her own mug for comfort.

'That was only initially. It was a shock when you first mentioned it, but when I saw the state it was in and how sympathetic your plans were, I soon came round to your way of thinking.' She looked across at him accusingly. 'You must have known it.'

He moved over to sit beside her on the settee. 'I find it impossible to know exactly what you *are* thinking, Becky. I enjoy working with you and you appear to enjoy working with me, but that seems to be as far as it goes. Whenever I try to take it further, something or someone comes between us. And if it's not Paddocks, I wish I knew what it was.'

His words had a sobering effect on Becky. Had she been wrong to be so jealous of him lunching with Rose? Perhaps it had been purely about work. She stared into her mug of coffee as if it would tell her how to answer. She knew only too well what he was asking, but how could she bring Julie into the conversation, knowing it would hurt him deeply?

'I love my work at Sandley, Marc, and I enjoy working with you all. Even Rose appears to tolerate me now.' She laughed. 'But...' She ground to a stop and, chickening out, improvised hastily, 'But I'm not sure I'm ready for anything more than a career at the moment.'

He removed her empty coffee mug gently from her hands and placed it on the table. Then, resting his hands gently on her shoulders, he turned her to look at him. 'That hasn't been my impression. Can you possibly deny your response to my kisses?'

'No Marc, I can't. But I'm only human and to be successful a relationship needs to be more than physical.'

He uttered a resigned sigh, before saying, 'As usual, we don't have time to continue this debate at the moment. It's already twelve-thirty and you have a mortgage to arrange. Is there anything I can do to help?'

Relieved that he wasn't asking any more of her, she shook her head. 'I don't think there'll be any problem, thanks. I've taken up far too much of your time already.' She rose lithely to her feet and said, 'I'll drop you home first.'

She thought he looked uneasy. 'There's no need. I can walk. But I do want to ask you something.'

'Yes?'

'Would you join me for a celebratory meal this evening?'

Still acutely aware of his disappointment over Paddocks she asked with a puzzled frown, 'Celebrating what?'

'Your first foray into home ownership.'

Becky felt a sudden elation surge through her and her smile must have told him her answer before she said the words. 'I'd love to, Marc.'

At last he had asked her to go out with him for a meal that wasn't by way of a thank-you for work done beyond the call of duty. Perhaps there was hope for them after all.

His sudden smile of satisfaction told her that he perhaps thought so, too. Had he at last thrown off his fear that anything he might enjoy would be cruelly snatched away from him?

She hardly dared believe it when he said, 'I'll pick you up here about seven. OK?'

'Fine. Are you sure I can't run you home?'

He shook his head vehemently. 'I need a walk in the air

to clear my head after such a heady cup of coffee. Thank goodness for that rain check you gave me.'

He laughed delightedly and, clasping his arms around her, swung her off her feet and round and round until she was so dizzy she could make no protest when he pulled her close and his lips moved to her mouth with a passion that threatened to keep them both prisoner for the remainder of the day.

He released her at length, and with a laughing pat on her behind said, 'If you don't go now, you'll lose your new home.'

His mood was so changed from when she had first met up with him that morning that Becky didn't want to go, but she tried to be sensible.

'If you're sure I can't drop you anywhere.'

He shook his head. 'If you have a chance, give me a ring when all your arrangements are complete, otherwise I'll be round about seven to finish what we have just begun.'

He strode off in the opposite direction to the town centre. Before she started the engine of her car, she watched him with an incredible feeling of warmth as she thought about the promise he had just made.

The thought of Marc taking even further his onslaught on her senses and her emotions was overwhelming, and for a moment the prospect made her too dizzy to drive. She was left with just one tinge of regret. She still had no idea where the house he had once shared with Julie was, and if wanting to keep it hidden from her was his reason for refusing a lift, was Julie still going to be a barrier between them?

Marc's feet didn't touch the pavement as he walked home. Three hours ago he had felt life wasn't worth living. He'd barely slept as he'd mulled over his disappointments. Losing all the work he'd put into the plans for Paddocks, that had been bad enough—but losing Becky, that had been worse. He wanted her and if his dreams when he finally had slept were anything to go by, he needed her—desperately.

But she hadn't seemed to want him. Despite the attraction he was sure she felt for him. Why? Even when he'd given her the good news about Alan Brown's house, she had tried to get out of him accompanying her.

As he'd waited on the doorstep of the cottage for first the agent and then Becky, he'd wondered what on earth he was doing there, making more of a fool of himself than he was already.

And then, when they'd seen the house and he had made up his mind to remove himself from her life, the sun that had been shining all morning had succeeded in penetrating his black mood. She had offered him that rain-check coffee which he had thought long forgotten. And the day had got better and better.

Her unexpected disappointment at losing Paddocks had given him the chance to open his heart to her, and though he still wasn't clear about her reasons for keeping him at arm's length he seemed to be finding a way round the obstacle.

Hopefully, tonight he would be able to convince her of his love for her. For he was in no doubt about it now. He loved her, and he intended to marry her just as soon as it could be arranged.

He'd been surprised at his mother's perception when he'd told her Becky had suggested she might like to take in that poor, ill-treated Labrador.

'She's a very caring girl. You could do a lot worse than marry her.'

'Mum!' he'd exclaimed. 'You've only met her the once.'

'And that was enough. I can read between the lines when

you talk about her. You love her and I want you to know that if I'm the reason you're doing nothing about it, I can assure you I don't mind in the least. I want to see you happily settled and producing some grandchildren before I'm too old to enjoy them.'

He'd been way off beam, thinking he needed to proceed with caution for his mother's sake. For the first time in five years he was free. His heart leapt painfully. If all went well, he would ask her to marry him that evening.

But first he needed to find out how she would feel about moving into the home he had shared with Julie.

If she objected, he would sell it. It was comfortable as modern houses went, but he no longer felt any sentimental attachment to it. Funny, that. When Julie died he had vowed never to part with it or change an item of the furnishing.

Meeting Becky, that had changed his feelings about the place completely. It was amazing what love could do.

CHAPTER TEN

THERE *was* a problem with the mortgage. When her account supervisor saw the price was quite a bit higher than the Snells had been asking, he felt that on her salary Becky was stretching herself too far.

'Perhaps you could reduce your offer?' he suggested.

'It difficult. I've been given first refusal.'

'I see. There's no chance you could raise a larger deposit, then?'

Becky couldn't see her way to doing that either. The only way would be to ask her mother for a loan, and although Becky knew she would help if she could, it wouldn't be easy and she didn't want to put her in that position.

'How about asking for a raise, then?' he quipped with the ease of someone not bound by pay restraint.

'I don't think that's an option either.'

'You do have a good banking record, so all I can suggest is that you fill in the forms and I'll chat it over with my manager and let you know our decision on Monday.'

Becky was despondent as she moved on to the supermarket to pick up the necessities to tide her over the weekend. Marc's invitation had left her on such a high that she hadn't believed anything could go wrong on this beautiful day. But the bad news at the bank had had the effect of making her wonder if her outing with Marc would turn sour on her as well.

It was mid-afternoon by the time she arrived home. She rang the estate agent and left a message on his answerphone to the effect that she was very interested in the house, but that she wasn't sure she could raise the asking price. She concluded by saying she would contact him as soon as she heard from the bank.

She wandered into the kitchen and switched on the kettle for a cup of coffee. She had been going to make herself a sandwich, but her appetite had vanished with her hopes.

The telephone disturbed her morose thoughts. It was Marc. 'Hi. You didn't ring. Any news?'

'Sorry, I've not been in long.' She tried to appear nonchalant. 'Unfortunately, the bank thinks I'm aiming just that bit too high.'

'That's unusual. I thought they were pushing money like it's going out of fashion.'

'The chap I saw hasn't rejected my application outright, but he has to consult a higher authority on Monday. I've left a message to that effect for the agent.'

'I'm sure it'll be all right. And you do know, don't you, that I'll help if you'll let me?' he offered in a solicitous voice.

'I'll manage,' she responded spiritedly. Although she guessed he could easily afford the small loan she needed, she didn't want to be in his debt. This was her venture and she wanted to go it alone.

'I know you'll manage, but if I can make that managing easier for you I'd like to do it,' he insisted. Then, obviously not expecting her to change her mind, he said, 'It's a beautiful afternoon, Becky. Let's make the most of what's left of it and drive down to the coast.'

'Sounds just what the doctor ordered,' she said with a giggle.

'I'm on my way.'

The happiness she had felt earlier flooded back, and she hugged to herself the thought of the time she was about to spend with him. Remembering his invitation to dinner, she wondered if she should change, or if they would be back in time to do so.

No problem. She would ask him when he arrived.

But he didn't come up to the flat, just announced his arrival with a toot of his horn. She ran lightly down the stairs and out to the car.

When she asked him about dressing for dinner, he shook his head. 'That's ideal for where I'm taking you and it's just right for me. You look so cool in that dress. I thought this morning how tempting you were and I've just realised how irresistible that temptation is.

'That's why I didn't come up to the flat,' he told her between the shower of kisses that accompanied his rapturous welcome. 'I knew we'd never enjoy this lovely sunshine if I did.'

They spent the remainder of the afternoon like carefree children, paddling in the sea and racing along the beach, falling into each other's arms exhausted as they reached the finishing point.

Becky didn't think she had ever been so happy, despite her disappointment over the mortgage.

As the sun began to dip, and the wind blew with a threatening chill, Marc checked his watch. 'I think it's time we should be moving.'

He took her hand and as they reluctantly turned from the water, a frantic screaming a little way down the beach made them turn.

A small boy on what appeared to be an inflatable duck was being carried rapidly out with the tide, while his two slightly older friends danced and screamed on the edge of the water.

Marc didn't hesitate. Loosing Becky's hand, he flung the shoes he was carrying towards her, and raced fully clothed into the water. He struck out rapidly in pursuit of the terrified child.

Becky watched. And held her breath. She searched the beach for help, but found none. The crowds, who only moments ago had been enjoying the sun, had disappeared—apart from an angry man, tightly clutching the two older children. His wife, beside him, was weeping copiously.

'Is there a phone?'

The woman gestured towards the mobile she was holding. 'I've rung. Police and ambulance are on their way.'

Becky searched the heaving water for a sight of Marc. The wind was too strong. It seemed to be carrying the inflatable increasingly out of his reach. Each time she thought he might catch hold of it, another gust swept the duck away.

She could see he was tiring. Every wave seemed to swamp his efforts. Every time he disappeared beneath the water she held her breath in panic until she saw his head emerge again.

With a sudden superhuman effort, he managed to grab the child, but the inflatable sailed off at an even faster rate.

There was still no sign of the emergency services and she could see he was exhausted as he turned towards them. The struggling bundle was clearly hampering his efforts to make headway against the receding tide.

She ran up the beach but could find no ropes, no lifebuoys. Nothing that might help.

She heard sirens in the distance and turned to monitor Marc's progress. She couldn't see him. Or the child. Screaming, she raced down and into the water. She was not a strong swimmer, but she had to do something. She couldn't let the happiness they had just found disappear.

Tears streaming down her cheeks, she paddled through ankle-deep water searching for some sign that he was still afloat.

'There, there,' the wailing woman screamed suddenly, and ran towards a wooden breakwater.

It seemed like hours until she spotted what the woman had seen. Marc must have been swept down the beach by a strong current and, still clutching the now quiet child, was attempting to clamber to his feet in shallow water.

As the woman snatched the child from him, police and paramedics flooded the beach. The toddler was immediately wrapped in a blanket and surrounded by the ambulance crew.

Becky ran through the water to where Marc lay, too exhausted to move.

Every breath Marc took excruciatingly seared his lungs. Every muscle in his body was screaming painfully for oxygen. He heard a deep voice ask, 'Are you all right, sir?' That was followed by Becky saying anxiously, 'Marc, Marc, say something.'

He tried unsuccessfully to open his eyes. Unable to find enough breath to speak, he inclined his head in a slight nod.

Becky took his hand, and he felt her hand gently smoothing back his hair. 'Oh, Marc. I thought I was going to lose you. I was so afraid.'

He squeezed her hand. He'd been scared, too. Not for himself, but for Becky. The thought of their newly found happiness being snatched away from them by the surging water was what had kept him struggling against all the odds.

As the paramedics carried her child up the beach, the still-weeping woman ran over to them. 'He's going to be all right. Thank you, oh, thank you so much,' she repeated over and over again, then said, 'I don't know how I can ever thank you enough.'

Marc was recovering sufficiently to raise himself to a

sitting position and say bluntly, 'By not allowing your children to play alone at the water's edge ever again.'

'I didn't, I didn't,' she cried. 'I told them only to play in that pool.' She pointed to a sizeable stretch of water left behind by the tide. 'I only turned my back for a second...'

Marc ignored her and struggled unsteadily to his feet. Becky grasped his arm.

'I'm going to get into some dry clothes.'

One of the hovering policeman said, 'You ought to be checked over at the hospital.'

'I'm fine,' he told them curtly, and started to make his way back to the car, pausing only to allow Becky to retrieve their footwear.

When they were out of earshot he muttered, 'That's all they ever do, turn their backs for a moment. That's all the rescue boat was supposed to have done, but Dad and Julie died.'

Realising there was a good reason for his unaccustomed rudeness, Becky said, 'If you take that wet shirt off, I've a woollen jacket in the car.'

'I'll be fine once the engine's running, but I'm afraid I'll have to go home and change.'

Becky replied with a hesitant grin, 'I didn't really expect you to sit through a meal like that.' She moved her arm around his waist. 'What you did was very brave, Marc. I really thought I'd lost you.' She shuddered at the thought.

He shrugged off both her arm and her compliment. 'You'll get that pretty dress soaked from my clothes. What I did wasn't brave. It's what I should have done for Dad and Julie.'

They had now reached the car and Becky's heart sank at his unyielding expression.

'But you weren't there, were you?' Becky queried gently.

'No, but I should have been.'

'How can you blame yourself?' she whispered, as he set the car in motion.

She watched the pain flash across his face and her heart sank like a stone, aware that this incident could undo all the progress she'd thought they'd made that morning.

She wanted to wrap her arms around him and help him to forget the nightmare his rescue had revived, but she couldn't while he was driving, and she wasn't even sure he would want her to.

'Julie hated the long hours I worked. The day she died she was angry with me for working another Saturday morning, and I was angry that she refused to understand that doctors can't work nine till five, weekdays only. We had a furious row and when I'd left for work she rang Dad and persuaded him to race with her that day.'

Becky swallowed hard. 'Oh, Marc. I'm so sorry…'

He seemed not to have heard. 'Dad enjoyed pottering in a boat, but he was never a racer. Julie must have persuaded him out of his depth, sailing-wise.'

She was lost in thoughts of what she could do to restore his earlier euphoric mood when the car stopped, jolting her back into the real world.

They were parked in a cul-de-sac of expensive detached houses, each with a double garage.

'Home,' he told her tersely. 'Number 23 Royal Court.'

She followed him into the house and felt immediately uncomfortable.

It was what she had wanted—to see where he lived. But not this way. After what had just happened, the house he had shared with Julie was the last place she could imagine restoring their earlier rapport.

He set off up the stairs then hesitated, 'The kitchen's through there—a cup of coffee would be wonderful.'

She filled the kettle, then searched the cupboards for coffee and mugs, but she felt increasingly uneasy doing so. This was another woman's home, which she had made with Marc, and Becky couldn't relax with the ghost of Julie looking over her shoulder.

She was tense when Marc came down dressed in a pair of light-coloured chinos and a dark red shirt. He took the mug of coffee she proffered and led the way through to the sitting room.

Becky looked round and knew intuitively that the decoration and furnishing had been Julie's choice, which only increased her personal conflict.

Her vague attempts to join in his one-sided conversation must have rattled him, for as soon as they'd finished the coffee he said they had to leave for their booked table.

They climbed into the car, and on the pretext of reaching for her seat belt he brushed her lips with a kiss so light it roused all her emotions.

Turning in her seat to face him, their eyes met, and for the first time she saw in his eyes a depth of sensitivity and desire that made her heart somersault as she realised he must have been acutely aware of her discomfort in the house but had waited until they were in the car to let her know.

He broke the spell, by fixing her belt and saying, 'If we're going to eat, I think we'd better leave this until later.' Smiling ruefully, he started the engine and, letting the clutch in smoothly, made for the main road.

As he drew into the car park of an old timber building built in the Elizabethan style, Becky gasped. It was small, but hundreds of tiny coloured lights gave it a fairy-tale appearance, and as they entered the front door she could see that the interior was also unspoilt. Low smoke-darkened beams gave the interior a warm and cosy appearance.

Becky turned excitedly to Marc. 'It's lovely. I only hope the food is as good as the surroundings.'

'I'm sure you'll find it is. I don't know what your favourite food is, Becky, but there's a good chance it'll be on the comprehensive menu here.'

Chatting like children in a hurry to discover everything they could about one another on first meeting, Becky hoped she was succeeding in making him forget the incident that had so cruelly marred the sunny afternoon.

As the seafood starters were served, she could no longer deny that the attraction which she had tried so hard to pretend didn't exist had already grown into love. She had fallen for him—heart, mind and soul. So much so that she was no longer beset by the fear that she might be repeating her mother's mistake.

His heart-wrenching looks, his easy wit, his bravery that afternoon and the way he cared about everybody and everything were all awesome, and she knew he would never do anything to hurt her.

But could she be sure he felt the same way? She had just seen that he had changed nothing in the house since Julie's time. That was surely a bad sign.

He might be grateful for her assisting him to rise above his fears and unhappiness, but was it love? Or, like Rose, would he just be grateful to her for her part in his rehabilitation?

The thought was unsettling but after a delicious main course of duck, cooked as a speciality of the house, Becky rested back in her chair, replete with the food and the knowledge that they had reached the stage where silence between them meant just as much, if not more, than the most intimate conversation. The bottle of Chablis they had shared had mellowed and relaxed her, and she felt comfortable in his company.

He smiled at her. 'Anything more to eat, Becky?'

She shook her head.

'I couldn't eat another thing, Marc, but I'd love a cup of coffee. And you ought to have one before you drive.'

He eyed her quizzically. 'You think so? You've consumed most of the bottle of wine, or didn't you realise?'

She shook her head. He must have filled her glass up repeatedly without her noticing, probably whilst she was listening raptly to his stories and jokes.

Suddenly apprehensive, she drank her coffee black, and gratefully accepted a refill.

When he had settled the bill he led her from the restaurant. As he opened the car door she felt again the ghost of Julie, looking over her shoulder, and shuddered.

He seemed to understand. As he was driving he said quietly, 'I didn't intend to ever take you to that house. I'd already made up my mind I was going to sell it and start afresh.'

She looked at him in consternation. 'You don't have to do that for me—'

'I'm not,' he broke in heatedly. 'I'm doing it for me.'

When he pulled up outside her flat, she was reluctant to ask him in for a nightcap. She knew only too well where it would lead, and before she allowed that to happen she needed time to herself. Time to try and decide if she could live with his love for Julie—and his guilt.

'I know we've used up your rain check, but—' Her offer of coffee was never made because his lips found hers, silencing her.

Unbelievably, he seemed to be so tuned in to her that he could read her mind because when he finally released her he said, 'I won't come up tonight, Becky. Although I love you with all my heart, and we've had a wonderful day together, I want us both to be sure before we make any commitment.'

She had been about to tell him how much she loved him, too, when his closing words tore at her heart. After their day together could he possibly be questioning *her* motives?

Or did he himself still have some reservations, despite his protestation that he loved her?

Before she could formulate the words she was searching for, he kissed her again, a sweet and gentle kiss that left her gasping for more, then he sprang from the car to open the passenger door for her.

'I'll ring you tomorrow, love.'

She heard him drive away when she reached the front door, and knew she had made a mistake not to detain him by force and try to resolve the difficulties that had kept them apart for too long.

Consequently, she didn't sleep for wondering what she could say to him the next day to convince him that nothing mattered but their love.

She had been up for hours when he rang the next morning. 'I've thought of a way out of your problem with the mortgage.'

'What's that?'

'I can't tell you. You'll have to come and see it.'

'When?'

'Now.'

Not having worked out a strategy that she believed would convince him, she prevaricated. 'I've a lot to catch up on. Couldn't we make it later?'

'Not really. I've arranged to take Mum to the kennels this afternoon to meet the Snells' cast-off, and I thought you might like to come with us.'

'I would. Very much.'

'I'll be round in ten minutes.'

She felt a growing excitement at his persistence. Wondering if he had found a house with a lower price tag, she dressed quickly and was waiting downstairs when he arrived.

His kiss of greeting was perfunctory and yet she read his excitement in it. However, she was surprised when he took the road to Marbury. 'I can't believe you've found a house in my price range around here.'

He gave her a secretive smile. 'I don't remember saying I'd found a house for you to buy. Wait and see.'

When he turned into the gateway to Paddocks, she exclaimed, 'I can't afford this!'

He hopped out to open the gate and on his return said to her, 'All I promised was a way to solve your problem.'

Puzzled now, she remained silent while he parked the car and unlocked the front door of the house. But when she was about to enter he stopped her, and sweeping her up into his arms, said, 'I have to carry you over the threshold.'

'Why?'

Before he restored her to her feet in the dusty entrance hall, he bent and kissed her. 'Because this is to be our new home. I put my house on the market this morning and put an offer in for this house that you always said should remain a home.'

'But—'

'Say nothing except that you'll marry me, Becky, so that we can live happily ever after at Paddocks.'

'Yes, oh, yes, please, Marc.' When it came down to it, she didn't have to give her answer a thought, apart from adding slyly, 'As long as you modernise the kitchen!'

He grinned. 'That goes without saying,' he murmured, before pressing a trail of hot, urgent kisses on her eyes, on her lips and down onto her neck and shoulders.

Eventually he held her away from him and said, 'Seems

like the bank and the members of the planning committee have done us both a good turn.'

She nodded happily as he whispered, 'I do so love you, Becky.'

Breathlessly she wrapped her arms around him and led him into her favourite utility room. She pulled him down beside her onto the wooden window-seat and, taking him in her arms, murmured gently, 'I know you loved Julie, Marc, and I'm not asking you to forget her. The happiness you shared with her is what has made you into the man I love today.' She pulled him close. 'And the man I want to make love to me. Starting—now!'

'Oh, Becky. I never expected to find such happiness again, and yesterday when I went home to change I really thought I'd blown any chance with you. You so hated being in the house that I'd shared with Julie, didn't you? I've been such a fool. Living there has prevented me from moving forward.'

She considered for a moment. 'You know, I thought I did. I sensed Julie's ghost hovering there, but I know now it wasn't because she resented my presence—it was because she wanted you to be happy again.'

As she lifted her face to his, she saw tears of happiness in his eyes. When he had sufficiently recovered his emotions, he murmured with a teasing glint in his eye, 'Just remember, it was you who dragged me down onto this seat. I refuse to take the blame again!'

Pulling away from him to look deep into his eyes, Becky smiled. 'I'm sorry, Marc. When we first met I didn't appreciate just how badly the past had affected you. I've been very unsure of what you expected of me. And until yesterday I don't believe you knew yourself.'

He seemed taken aback. 'What about you? You took

great delight in fending me off if I dared to get too close. Was I meant to read that as a sign of your affection?'

Becky smiled and hesitantly explained how the events of her early childhood had affected every one of her romantic liaisons. 'Until now! That's why Paddocks meant so much to me. It was the only place I knew Mum was safe from Dad and I could be happy.'

'What happened to your father?'

She shrugged. 'He moved away while we were living at Paddocks. I never saw him again and neither did Mum. The last she heard he was living abroad.'

'How dreadful for her. And she didn't marry again?'

Becky raised a cynical eyebrow. 'You must be joking. She had more reason to distrust marriage than I did. No. She brought me up alone.'

'That can't have been easy.'

'It was easier than living *with* him, I can tell you.'

The look he gave her as he pulled her towards him was full of sympathy and tenderness. After he had taken her lips mercilessly, he murmured, 'I promise never to do anything that will make you feel that way about me.' He gave her a sly grin. 'Unless, of course, my making love to you at every opportunity will?'

She lifted her lashes and, looking up into his dark clear eyes which she suddenly realised, had no longer anything to hide, she whispered, 'I don't think that'll be a problem, do you?'

Holding his face firmly between her hands, Becky silenced his reply by giving his lips something else to do.

MILLS & BOON®

Makes any time special

Enjoy a romantic novel from
Mills & Boon®

Presents...™   *Enchanted™*   TEMPTATION.

Historical Romance™   ⊣MEDICAL ROMANCE™

THE GIRL NEXT DOOR by Caroline Anderson
Audley Memorial Hospital

When surgeon Nick Sarazin and his two children, Ben and Amy, moved next door to ward sister Veronica Matthews, she helped as much as possible. It was clear to Ronnie that Nick had yet to let go of his wife's memory, and there'd only be heartache, loving this beautiful man...

THE MARRIAGE OF DR MARR by Lilian Darcy
Southshore # 3 of 4

Dr Julius Marr had been deeply impressed by Stephanie Reid's care of her mother, but afterwards he didn't know how to stay in touch—until he could offer her the job of receptionist at the practice. But until he'd tied up some loose ends, they couldn't move forward.

DR BRIGHT'S EXPECTATIONS by Abigail Gordon

Nurse Antonia Bliss first met paediatrician Jonathan Bright when she was dressed as the Easter Bunny! Was that why he thought she couldn't know her own mind? But his own expectations were so battered, he needed some excuse to keep her at a distance...

0002/03a

Available from 3rd March 2000

Available at most branches of WH Smith, Tesco, Martins, Borders, Easons, Volume One/James Thin and most good paperback bookshops

MILLS & BOON®

MEDICAL ROMANCE™

A SON FOR JOHN by Gill Sanderson
Bachelor Doctors

Since qualifying Dr John Cord had concentrated on work,
trying to forget that he had loved and lost his Eleanor. But
his new Obs and Gynae job brought her back into his life.
Even more shocking was the sight of a photo on Ellie's desk
of a young boy who was clearly his son!

IDYLLIC INTERLUDE by Helen Shelton

Surgeon Nathan Thomas borrowed his step-brother's
Cornish cottage, only to find himself next door to a
beautiful girl. Not one to poach, Nathan was horrified by his
instant attraction to nurse Libby Deane, assuming she was
Alistair's girlfriend.

AN ENTICING PROPOSAL by Meredith Webber

When nurse Paige Warren rescued a young Italian woman,
she phoned Italy leaving a message for 'Marco', but Dr
Marco Alberici—an Italian prince!—arrives in person,
disrupting her surgery and her hormones! Should she really
accept his invitation to return to Italy?

0002/0

Available from 3rd March 2000

FREE!

4 Books
and a surprise gift!

We would like to take this opportunity to thank you for reading this Mills & Boon® book by offering you the chance to take FOUR more specially selected titles from the Medical Romance™ series absolutely FREE! We're also making this offer to introduce you to the benefits of the Reader Service™—

- ★ FREE home delivery
- ★ FREE gifts and competitions
- ★ FREE monthly Newsletter
- ★ Books available before they're in the shops
- · ★ Exclusive Reader Service discounts

Accepting these FREE books and gift places you under no obligation to buy; you may cancel at any time, even after receiving your free shipment. Simply complete your details below and return the entire page to the address below. ***You don't even need a stamp!***

YES! Please send me 4 free Medical Romance books and a surprise gift. I understand that unless you hear from me, I will receive 6 superb new titles every month for just £2.40 each, postage and packing free. I am under no obligation to purchase any books and may cancel my subscription at any time. The free books and gift will be mine to keep in any case.

MOEB

Ms/Mrs/Miss/Mr ....Initials ....
BLOCK CAPITALS PLEASE

Surname...

Address..

....

....Postcode ....

Send this whole page to:
UK: The Reader Service, FREEPOST CN81, Croydon, CR9 3WZ
EIRE: The Reader Service, PO Box 4546, Kilcock, County Kildare (stamp required)

Offer not valid to current Reader Service subscribers to this series. We reserve the right to refuse an application and applicants must be aged 18 years or over. Only one application per household. Terms and prices subject to change without notice. Offer expires 31st August 2000. As a result of this application, you may receive further offers from Harlequin Mills & Boon Limited and other carefully selected companies. If you would prefer not to share in this opportunity please write to The Data Manager at the address above.

Mills & Boon is a registered trademark owned by Harlequin Mills & Boon Limited.
Medical Romance is being used as a trademark.